# Schemes to the Heart

by Madeline Quinn

The Heart's Price series

Book 1

A Note from the Author:

*Schemes to the Heart* is a retelling of *Enticing the Boss*, an erotic novella now out of print, published by this author under the pen name Lily Bly through The Wild Rose Press, Inc. All rights have been returned to the author. The title has been changed, the erotic scenes have been toned down to slow-burn romance, and the path between the main characters has been elongated.

*There's a certain slant of light,*
*On winter afternoons,*
*That oppresses, like the weight*
*Of cathedral tunes.*

*Heavenly hurt it gives us ;*
*We can find no scar,*
*But internal difference*
*Where the meanings are.*

*None may teach it anything,*
*'T is the seal, despair, —*
*An imperial affliction*
*Sent us of the air.*

*When it comes, the landscape listens,*
*Shadows hold their breath ;*
*When it goes, 't is like the distance*
*On the look of death.*

## ~ Emily Dickinson

Dickinson, Emily. Poems by Emily Dickinson. Roberts Brothers, Boston, 11 ed., 1892. p. 106. Accessed on Google
    Books.

*This book is dedicated to*
*anyone who believes*
*they don't deserve*
*a happily-ever-after.*

# Prologue

*Beth*

"Jeanie! Jeanie! I dream of Jeanie!" I led the jeering chorus, my voice sharp and shrill, echoing off the brick walls of the school. My fingers curled around the neck of a plastic pop bottle, sticky with the remnants of cheap soda, and I hurled it with all the pent-up anger I could muster. The others followed me, laughing, pelting the little wimp with whatever trash they could find. The quad, usually a bland, sun-bleached expanse of concrete and worn-out benches, was alive with the cruel energy of the mob.

Jean tried to shield herself with her backpack, a too-bright pink against the drab gray of the day, its edges frayed from heavy trips to school and the library. She stumbled away, her gangly, skinny legs pumping like she could outrun the inevitable. But she couldn't. No one ever could. She tripped on the uneven lip of the sidewalk and sprawled onto the muddy grass, her face a mask of shock and humiliation. A sprinkler whirred to life, spraying her with cold water, soaking her torn jeans and sweater. She looked so pathetic, spread-eagled like some kind of discarded, forgotten doll, dirt-streaked and drenched, red hair plastered to her cheeks.

What would Mom think of her now? Mom, who always gushed over Jean's straight As, her perfectly polished manners, her "bright future." There wouldn't be any of that why-can't-you-be-more-like-Jean crap if she could see this worthless, pitiful mess now. Stupid little seventh grader. In Mom's eyes, Jean was nothing but a walking, talking reminder of everything I'd never be. But today, she was just a soggy, muddied wreck.

"Guess what? No one will ever dream of you, Jeanie!" I shouted, my voice breaking into a harsh cackle. I knew she hated that name. It crawled under her skin, just like I did.

Stupid little Jean. I hated her guts. She had everything handed to her—everything I never got. Mom didn't marry her dad for love; she married him for his money. And all I got out of the deal were two spoiled, pampered step-siblings who never had to work a day for anything. George was older, in college, far away, where he could live up to every expectation I'd never meet. But Jean, she was stuck here. And as long as she was, I'd make her life hell.

I snatched the last pop bottle from the kid beside me, my fingers tight around the flimsy plastic, and I hurled it with everything I had. It struck her square in the face as she tried to stand. A sharp, satisfying smack echoed in my ears.

"Mr. Wilson!" the lookout yelled, and we scattered like roaches in the light. The geometry teacher pretended he cared but never really did. He charged down the walkway, his face a twisted scowl of useless authority.

I turned to run, adrenaline coursing hot and fierce, but I couldn't help glancing back. Jean was on her hands and knees on the ground, her face streaked with tears and dirt, but it wasn't the crying that got me. It was her gaze. She was staring straight at me, not with anger or fear, but with something far worse. *Pity*.

My stomach churned, a cold, bitter knot forming as I realized it wasn't self-pity in her eyes—it was pity for me.

*Me*.

She thought I was the pathetic one. The loser. And I couldn't stand it. Not for a second.

I promised myself that she'd get what was coming to her one day. She was going to pay for looking at me like that. She was going to get it, all right.

# Chapter One

*Jean*

*Seventeen Years Later*

I double-checked the backup software running on my computer, watching as the familiar loading bar crept slowly across the screen. The hum of the tower's fan was the only sound in my office, an unsettling reminder of the late hour. The hallway lights had dimmed to their energy-saver mode hours ago, casting faint blue pools of light that flickered and buzzed faintly. I rubbed the back of my neck, feeling the tension still knotted there, and tried to remind myself that it was okay to go on my vacation. I straightened a final stack of papers, aligning their edges with meticulous care, as if by perfecting this small task, everything else would just fall in line.

"Shep and Son will survive without me for a week," I muttered, my voice breaking the heavy silence. The words lacked conviction as I glanced around the office that had become more of a home to me than my suburban two-bedroom.

"I've taken one vacation in six years. Time for some *me* time." I exhaled, slowly and deliberately, the way yoga classes teach for centering. But all it did was fan the familiar guilt creeping back in.

My vacation was *not*, I insisted again, an act of avoidance. It wasn't about the upcoming engagement party—that perfectly staged spectacle of David and Beth's happiness. It wasn't. That incredible ski package to Skypoint, Colorado, had appeared as if by magic, a last-minute deal too good to pass up. If it hadn't been for the plans laid out with my brother and niece months ago, I would have no problem attending the engagement party. I'd be there, plastering on a smile, raising a glass to my boss and step-sister's happiness, and pretending that every toast didn't feel like a large gauge needle stabbing my heart. I'd eat cake and maybe even deliver some witty speech wishing them all the best—a speech carefully crafted, as only an editor could, to express the precise amount of measured goodwill appropriate for the occasion.

"Yes," I told my empty office, aligning sticky notes with the edges of manuscript excerpts. "I would definitely do that—*if* I was going to be here." But instead, I'd be on a plane, soaring high above all the drama, heading toward snow-covered mountains and crisp, cold air that promised escape.

I pulled my salt-and-pepper wool coat from the hook next to my framed favorite Emily Dickinson poem on the wall. It settled comfortably around me in a hug. I tugged on my gloves and swung my purse over my shoulder. Still, a horrifying prediction persisted in my mind—me hiding in the supply closet at the party, stuffing my tear-stained face with leftover cake while everyone else basked in the glow of David and Beth's perfect romance.

"No," I told myself more forcefully, trying to shake off the frown that tugged at the corners of my mouth. "I will be skiing through a beautiful alpine vista on Monday morning with George and Mary." The words sounded rehearsed, like a line I'd been practicing in the mirror. I needed to believe it. I had to. Something in that mountain air would cleanse me, rid me of this lingering infatuation with David Shep once and for all. Come June, he would be someone else's problem. He was off the market now—engaged. To Beth Oakley.

My heart tightened at the thought, a familiar ache that I couldn't quite swallow. Why did it have to be Beth? It was like the universe's cruel joke, twisting a knife over and over again in a wound that never fully healed but somehow wasn't critical enough to actually do me in. I felt immense empathy for Prometheus and his liver.

My throat constricted, and I fought against the surge of old, bitter emotions. I tapped the Pennywise Killer Clown bobblehead perched on my desk, watching as it swayed back and forth. Its grotesque grin and wide, menacing eyes were so out of place amidst my sleek, contemporary office decor, but it served as a personal talisman. Its presence felt like a small victory. Had I known Beth suffered from coulrophobia back when we were kids, maybe things would've been different between us. Maybe I would have gained the upper hand every once in a while.

As it was, Beth hadn't set foot in my office since I placed Pennywise facing the door, its unsettling stare always positioned to greet her like an unwelcoming host. Even George had once told me it was cruel, but he didn't know the half of it. To him, it was just a funny little prank. To me, it was a symbol of reclaiming space.

Supposedly Beth and I had put everything behind us. We were adults now, grown women who were meant to be civil, if not friendly. "I just happen to like Stephen King," I'd told David once when he'd asked about the bobblehead, forcing a casual smile. "We're in the publishing business. Who doesn't dream of finding the next king of horror?"

Or the next king of anything, really. Because Shep and Son was in trouble, and we all knew it. The publishing house had been a beacon for the new and different for decades, but the last few years had hit us hard. It was sink or swim, and Monday's pitch to Frederick Donelson—a billionaire with a penchant for wild, self-aggrandizing adventures—was our last, best shot. If we could land him, the seven-book deal might just keep us afloat. It was a high-stakes game, and Shep and Son was counting on it.

I stepped carefully across the carpeted floor of my office, the high heels I'd chosen this morning causing my feet to ache. They were cute, no doubt, and they made my legs look great—elevated, sculpted from the gym's latest brutal squat session—but I was paying for it now. "Like one pair of shoes and a nice butt is going to have more effect on David Shep than six years of dedication," I muttered under my breath, feeling the sting of blisters forming. "Big brain move, Ivy League."

I was so caught up in my internal dialogue, lost in the sound of my own self-criticism, that I nearly missed the light spilling out of David's office. He'd been out most of the week, buried in meetings, and it wasn't like him to be around this late. I reached into the office, intending to flick off the forgotten light, but when I stepped inside, I found David there, hunched over his desk like a man bearing the weight of the world on his shoulders.

The usual polished, composed David was gone. His golden-brown hair—normally combed in perfect order—was disheveled, messy, with stray strands sticking up as though he'd run his hands through it one too many times in frustration. Papers were scattered everywhere, turning his normally organized desk into a sea of chaos. Hasty scribbles covered whiteboards with barely legible charts and numbers.

My fingers itched to smooth his hair, to offer some kind of comfort I wasn't sure I had the right to give. I swallowed hard against the impulse.

"David?" My voice was soft, but it still startled him.

His head jerked up, his eyes hazy, and for a moment, I wasn't sure he even recognized me. When he finally spoke, he exhaled my name like it was a lifeline. "Jean."

The way he said it sent a small thrill through me, something warm and undeniable. I tried to ignore the way my heart fluttered at the sound. I took a few steps closer, noting how David's appearance, hair mussed, shirt wrinkled and buttoned out of line, was reflected in the disorder around him. File drawers hung open like gaping mouths in the corner of the office, folders crammed in at odd angles, and every surface was littered with pages, many stained with coffee cup imprints.

"I didn't expect to see you here this late," I said, adjusting the strap of my purse and smoothing my coat lapel. David tried to smile, but it was weak. His lips barely lifted before they fell back into a defeated line. He sighed, running a hand over his face, the exhaustion etched deep in the lines around his eyes.

"Beth dumped me."

The words were blunt, delivered with a kind of hollow finality that stunned me. My breath caught, and for a second, I couldn't quite process it. David and Beth were the couple that everyone loved to hate, the kind who always seemed destined for that nauseatingly perfect happily-ever-after. They were the golden couple, and Beth had the ring to prove it. My mind spun as I tried to reconcile that image with the reality in front of me.

"What happened?" The disbelief was clear in my voice.

David leaned back in his chair, picking up a pencil and twirling it absently between his fingers. He looked like a man adrift, caught in the riptide of his own emotions. "She said I'd become too boring," he muttered, bitterness lacing his tone. "All work and no play or something. I guess my paying for her little fantasy life wasn't enough if I wasn't a constant part of it." He tossed the pencil, and it skittered across the desk, rolling to the floor. He rubbed his temples, his eyes clouded with frustration and something deeper—something that looked like regret.

My heart twisted, caught between the ugly satisfaction of seeing Beth falter and the genuine pain radiating from David. It was a complicated knot of jealousy and empathy, tangled with the old, unshakable truth that I wanted him to be happy, even if it wasn't with me. But seeing him like this, defeated and lost,

I couldn't help but wish I could somehow rewrite his story.

"After Dad's stroke, I just took on so much more," David continued, his voice cracking slightly. "And I…I thought Beth understood, but maybe she never did."

I tried to find the right words, something that would soothe the jagged edges of his hurt, but everything I came up with felt hollow. Edgar Shep had been more than just a boss to me; he'd been a mentor, a guiding force at Shep and Son. His sudden stroke two months ago had turned everything upside down, and the weight of his absence still lingered in all corners and six floors of the company. I'd been the one to find him, collapsed next to the desk in his office, and the memory still haunted me in quiet moments. I couldn't begin to imagine what it was like for David.

"I'm sorry," I said finally, my voice thick with unspoken apologies and my inability to fix an unfixable situation. "I knew you took on a lot more, but I didn't realize how much."

David's gaze met mine, the pain in his eyes stark and unguarded. For a brief, electrifying second, I thought I saw something there—a flash of connection, of unspoken understanding—but it passed too quickly to grasp.

"You're more supportive than I deserve," he said, his voice softening, and I felt the faintest flicker of something I hadn't allowed myself to hope for. I wanted to reach out, to close the distance between us, but I forced myself to stay rooted to the spot. He was hurting, vulnerable, and whatever I thought I saw was just the ghost of something that could never be.

"What's all this?" I asked, needing to break the tension that threatened to swallow us both. I gestured to the mess of papers sprawled across his desk, picking up a few stained pages.

David pulled at his earlobe, looking away. "The Donelson pitch," he said, his voice tight. "I'm behind. Way behind." He hesitated, guilt creeping into his expression. "I didn't realize how much until tonight."

The Donelson pitch was a point of contention between us. Three months ago, Edgar had initially made me lead on the project, but David protested. His dissent hadn't been evident from the start though, and I had my suspicions that Beth had pushed him to fight for it after she found out how huge the deal would be for the company. David pressed Edgar, and Edgar had come to me asking if I would mind giving up point to David. I could tell Edgar was proud that his only son seemed to be stepping up to the plate, but I also saw the hesitation there. I told Edgar that I would move back and just be available to help out however David needed. David, though, had guarded the project closely and never allowed my input or assistance of any kind.

"How far behind?" I guarded my tone.

He stood, placing his palms flat on the desk's mess. "I'm twenty-five percent done." He shrugged his shoulders and sucked a sharp breath in between grit teeth. "Maybe thirty."

My breath hitched, alarm bells in my head ringing. This was not the David Shep I knew—the man who could juggle a dozen projects with effortless charm. But I could see it now: cracks in his armor, strain from trying to keep everything together, personal and professional.

"David, this could break the company," I said, my voice rising with urgency. "We need this."

"I know." He paced the room, his movements restless, hands clenching and unclenching at his sides. "I know."

I could feel his anxiety, thick and palpable, hanging between us like a storm cloud. I wanted to shake him, to demand the reason why he hadn't asked for help sooner, but I bit back the words.

Instead, I made a decision. I dropped my purse and shrugged out of my coat, tossing it into a heap on the nearest chair. "Okay," I said, unbuttoning and rolling up the sleeves of my blouse. "Let's get to work. We've got sixty hours to turn this around."

David looked at me, surprise flickering in his eyes. "But your trip—"

"It's fine," I cut him off, pulling out my phone and quickly typing a text to my brother.

*Work emergency. Go to Colorado without me.*

George's response was instant, and I could almost hear his exasperated tone.

*Don't do this to yourself!*

I ignored him, shoving the phone back into my purse.

David hesitated, guilt tugging at the corners of his mouth. "Jean, I don't want you to give up your vacation because I screwed up."

I placed a hand on his sleeve, giving his arm a gentle squeeze. "We'll get through this. Together." The tension in David's shoulders eased, and as we dove into the chaos of the pitch, I saw a flicker of his usual self—determined, driven, the man I'd admired and secretly loved for far too long.

As we worked through the night, our laughter mingled with moments of quiet intensity. I couldn't help but think that maybe, just maybe, we were finally on the same page.

***

We had worked through Friday night, pacing the carpeted floor of his office, our footsteps soft and slow, the rhythm of two people locked in shared determination. The city outside had long gone to sleep, and the silence inside the building felt heavy, like we were the last two souls left awake in the world.

By one a.m., our shoes were discarded in a corner, and we

moved in stockinged feet, tiptoeing between stacks of papers and scattered notes as if afraid to disturb the tenuous calm that had settled between us. The whiteboards were a mess of scribbled ideas, numbers, and half-formed thoughts—our collective brainstorm sprawled out like a mind map of desperation.

Around seven a.m., exhaustion clung to us like a damp second skin, but we pressed on. I found myself in the staff lounge, filling the coffee pot for what felt like the hundredth time, the faucet's slow, steady trickle testing my already frayed patience. I stifled a yawn, covering my mouth with the back of my hand. The hours had blurred together in a haze of numbers and coffee stains.

David appeared behind me, reaching into the cupboard above the sink for the coffee grounds and filter. His arm brushed against my shoulder, a light, accidental touch, but it sent a jolt through me, my skin suddenly hyper-aware of every inch where we made contact. I leaned back slightly, and my shoulder met the solid expanse of his chest. I blinked rapidly, caught off guard by the sudden intimacy, and inhaled sharply. The familiar mix of his scent—spicy soap, a lingering trace of cologne, and a hint of sweat—flooded my senses. I squeezed my eyes shut, trying to compose myself against the surge of feelings I'd been suppressing for years.

"A little stronger this time?" His breath brushed against my ear, warm and close, sending a shiver down my spine. There was a softness in his tone, an invitation to linger in this uncharted territory we'd stumbled into.

"Hmm?" My voice was barely a murmur, as if speaking too loudly might break whatever fragile spell had wrapped itself around us. I kept my eyes closed and allowed myself the smallest luxury of leaning back into him more fully, feeling the steady rise and fall of his chest. It was reckless, letting the moment stretch a fraction longer than necessary, but my fatigue made me bold in ways I couldn't explain.

David's fingers brushed the hem of my untucked blouse, a light, tentative touch that sent sparks shooting across my skin. After a moment's hesitation, his hand settled on my hip, the pressure firm and possessive. "The coffee," he clarified, but the words seemed secondary, his focus entirely on the slow dance of proximity between us.

"What about the coffee?" I asked absently, my mind miles away from caffeine and creamer. It felt like we were teetering on the edge of something dangerous, a line I'd avoided crossing—but dreamt about—for so long. I leaned back a little more, testing the limits, and his grip tightened around the curve of my hip, anchoring me there.

"Do you want stronger coffee this time?" His voice dropped

lower, laced with a quiet intensity that made my pulse quicken. The night, the exhaustion, the weight of our shared efforts—it all seemed to converge in this moment, making the air between us thick and electric.

"Definitely," I whispered, hardly recognizing the breathy notes of my voice. It was more than the coffee; it was the promise of something we couldn't quite name but were both too exhausted to resist.

Cold water overflowed out of the coffee pot and snapped me out of the moment as. I jerked forward, startled, my heart racing as reality reasserted itself. David sprang back as well, bumping into the break-room table, the coffee can clattering to the floor from his hand with a metallic clang. The sound echoed like a warning bell, yanking us back to the present, to the boundaries we'd been skirting all night.

A key scraped in the lock, and the buzzer over the employee entrance sounded. "Burning the all-night oil again, eh, Miss Jean?" Sophie's sing-song voice rang out from the back hallway, breaking our tension. I lifted one foot out of the mess of coffee grounds, trying to regain my composure.

"Yes," I called out, my voice strained as I turned off the faucet, pouring the excess water from the coffee pot down the sink. My cheeks burned, a mix of embarrassment and something else—something I refused to name but that pulsed

17

hot and insistent under my skin.

David knelt to retrieve the coffee can, and his hand brushed my calf briefly, sending another ripple of awareness through me. I glanced down, catching the flicker of something in his eyes—hunger, longing, or maybe just the raw vulnerability of a moment caught off guard.

"I always know it's you." Sophie's voice grew louder as she neared the lounge, her cheerful obliviousness a jarring contrast to the charged silence that lingered between us. David straightened, stepping away from me, using visible effort to regain his usual composure. "Mr. Shep could learn a few things from you about— Oh! Hello, Mr. Shep."

"Hi, Sophie." David's response was polite as she stepped into the lounge, but there was a tightness to his posture. I busied myself with the coffee maker, trying to focus on anything but the residual heat of David's touch.

"I'll use the vacuum when you're done with it," David said, his voice returning to its usual controlled cadence. "We had a little mishap with the coffee here."

"Sure thing." Sophie's gaze lingered on me for a moment, a knowing smile tugging at her lips, and I wondered what she saw—two tired colleagues or something more?

"What is it I could learn from Jean?" David asked, his tone laced with forced casualness.

Sophie laughed, the sound light and unassuming. "Oh, I just wonder if you know how dedicated she is. She's here almost every Saturday that I am, but usually not quite so early—or late, depending on how you look at it." She turned to leave. "I'll get the vacuum from the closet," she called over her shoulder.

I forced a smile, even as my stomach twisted. I dumped what was left of the coffee grounds into the filter, my hands moving automatically. "Looks like we're going to need some more coffee," I said, tossing David a sidelong glance, half-expecting him to finally see through the carefully constructed facade I'd built around myself. Did he see how much of my life was tied up in this place? Did he realize what a workaholic loser I felt like sometimes, sacrificing weekends and personal moments for the hollow comfort of the office?

"Almost every Saturday?" David asked, his brows furrowing as he studied me, the weight of his gaze pressing down on the flimsy excuses my tired brain formulated to hide behind.

I wrinkled my nose and looked away, pretending to be engrossed in the coffee maker's buttons. "Well, no, just every now and then. I do have a life outside of the office." The words came out sharper than I intended, tinged with a defensiveness I hadn't meant to show.

"Sure," he said, his voice softer, as if he sensed the

undercurrent of truth I was trying to keep buried. "We all do."

"Yep." I poked the BREW NOW button with more force than necessary, and the click of the plastic echoed in the quiet. I stepped back, brushing at the coffee grounds clinging to my nylons, feeling the grit scratch against my skin. "Let's get back to work. Did you find any snacks?" I asked, trying to steer us back into safer, less vulnerable territory.

David gestured toward the sad selection of snacks on the table. "A half-eaten bag of pretzels and some corn nuts. Not exactly a feast."

I managed a weak laugh. "After Jerry's rotten egg incident last fall, everyone usually tries to clear out food before the weekend. Maybe I'll run out and grab us something—and some more coffee."

Sophie reappeared, pushing the vacuum into the lounge. "I can clean that up, Mr. Shep." She set her cleaning supplies on the floor, eyeing the mess of coffee grounds with a practiced eye.

"That's okay. I'll do it." David pulled out his wallet, extracting a fifty-dollar bill. "Would you mind running down to that all-night grocery store on Pinehurst for another can of coffee and some danishes? Maybe grab us a couple of cappuccinos from the gas station, too. You like hazelnut with a shot of vanilla, right, Jean?"

I nodded, a bit taken aback that he remembered. The small

detail felt oddly intimate, a reminder of the many mornings we'd collected our orders from bulk coffee runs before starting staff meetings.

"No problem." Sophie accepted the cash with a smile and a playful salute. She winked at me as she left, leaving us alone in the lounge again. David busied himself unwinding the vacuum's cord, and I couldn't help but watch the way his shoulders tensed with a quiet earnestness.

I went to the staff restroom and took off my nylons, relieved of their constriction and the grit of the coffee grounds. I dropped them into the garbage can and stared at myself in the mirror. The fluorescent bathroom light cast harsh shadows, deepening the hollows under my eyes and highlighting every flaw I had tried to cover up my entire life. My hair, a wild mess of red waves, framed my face in a way that felt both familiar and foreign, like a crown of copper that never sat quite right. I hated how it caught the light, turning me into a walking beacon, impossible to hide. I never had a say in the matter; I was born with those blazing locks, a genetic curse that screamed for attention I had never wanted. But every time I'd dyed through the years, it looked even worse, so I'd learned to live with it.

And then there were the freckles—those damn spots that spread across my nose and cheeks like a constellation of flaws. People said they were cute, like a splash of sun-kissed charm, but I knew better. They were just another marker of my difference, little spots that stubbornly refused to blend in, no matter how much concealer I smeared on them.

I traced my finger along the mirror, hovering over my reflection, trying to see past the exhaustion that had settled deep into my bones after 24 sleepless hours. The woman in the glass looked soft, almost delicate, but there was a defiance in the green of my eyes that I couldn't hide.

When I exited the bathroom, I could hear the vacuum still running in the lounge, and I headed back to David's office. I scanned the whiteboard numbers and notes, and my heart sank suddenly as I spotted a glaring error in our work. The realization hit me like a punch, the miscalculation glaringly obvious in the early morning light. I turned, startled, when I realized David had entered the office, his expression heavy with something unresolved.

"Jean, I—" He started, his voice low, the unspoken lingering between us.

I held up a hand to stop him, my other hand gesturing to the whiteboard. "Look at those sales coefficients. Where did we get those? They should be much higher." I reached for the papers strewn across the desk, my focus snapping back to the task at hand. The brief, stolen moment in the lounge faded, replaced by the relentless urgency of our work.

David's face fell, the heat in his gaze cooling into frustration. "Oh, crap," he muttered, running a hand through his disheveled hair. "This affects the entire pitch."

"Exactly," I said, the weight of the night—and everything we hadn't said—settling heavily between us once more. Twelve of our 60 hours gone.

***

*Beth*

I gripped the steering wheel, my knuckles white as I cruised past the Shep and Son office for the third time. The parking lot looked exactly the same—David's black truck next to Jean's white crossover, both of them sporting the dusting of snow from last night like they hadn't moved since they'd been parked Friday morning. My stomach twisted as I stared at the tinted office building's windows, half-expecting to see some hint of what they were doing in there. Thirty-one hours. That's how long it had been since I dumped him, expecting him to beg me to come back, to realize he couldn't live without me. But instead, he was in there with Jean, holed up for an entire night like they had nothing better to do but work. It was infuriating. Why could he possibly need to spend that much time with her? Jean, the mealy-mouthed ninny who buried her nose in books and made-up stories, had no business being that close to David.

I slowed down, glaring at the office, my heart thudding in

my chest. I could feel the anger bubbling up, mixing with something else that I hated to admit: jealousy. How pathetic was that? Jean was nothing. She was plain, boring, and always so damn serious. She didn't know how to have fun, how to let loose. Hell, she barely knew how to dress herself. She was just some background fixture in David's life. And yet, there he was, spending all his time with her, like she was suddenly important.

I turned the corner and pulled into a nearby parking lot, keeping my eyes on the office. I wanted to see something, anything, that would explain why David hadn't bothered to call me begging to reconsider our breakup, why he was choosing to waste his time with *her*. But the minutes ticked by, and nothing happened. It was like the world had gone on without me, and I was stuck on the outside looking in.

The truth was, I only started pursuing David to get under Jean's skin. I'd seen the way she looked at him—like he was the sun and she was some sad little flower desperate for light. It was pathetic. Jean was head over heels, and I could see it in every shy smile, every time she went out of her way to do something special for him. It made me sick.

So, I had set my sights on David. It wasn't difficult. He was good-looking, successful, and let's face it, he wasn't exactly immune to a little attention from a woman who knew how to get what she wanted. I went after him because I knew it would hurt Jean.

But then, I actually started to like him. He had a way of making me feel special, taking me to places I'd never been, giving me a glimpse of a life I'd never really considered. I liked the way he made me feel, the way he looked at me, and for a while, it was perfect.

But lately, he'd been distant, buried in work, and I was starting to feel like an afterthought. I tried talking to him about it, tried to make him see that I needed more from him, but all he did was brush me off. Yesterday, I finally confronted him, telling him he wasn't spending enough time with me. I thought he'd apologize, maybe make some grand gesture to show me I was still his priority.

But instead, he laughed. Actually laughed in my face and said, "I work for a living, Beth. It's not like playing with hair all day like you do." The words cut me like a knife, and the sting of them was still fresh, lingering like a bruise that wouldn't heal. He knew how hard I worked to build my career, how much I'd put into my stylist business, and he just dismissed it like it was nothing. Like I was nothing.

I slammed my fist against the steering wheel, the pain sharp and satisfying. Who the hell did he think he was? I'd worked harder than he had, clawing my way up from community college to build a life I could be proud of. Not like Jean and

George and their stupid scholarships or David and his daddy's money.

And now, David was in there with Jean, treating her like she was something special, like she was worth more than me. It made my skin crawl.

I fumbled for my phone in my purse, my fingers shaking as I pulled up David's contact. I stared at his name, my thumb hovering over the call button. Part of me wanted to scream at him, to remind him of what he was missing, but I couldn't bring myself to do it. No, I wasn't going to give him the satisfaction of knowing how much this was getting to me. If he wanted to play this game, then fine. I could play it better.

The sun was starting to set, casting the winter sky in hues of pink and orange, but I barely noticed. I was too busy fuming, imagining all the ways Jean was probably worming her way into David's head, acting like she was indispensable. She was probably telling him how hard she was working, how much she was doing for him, hoping he'd see her as more than just an employee.

But I knew better. Jean was nothing without her spreadsheets and her books, and David was just too blind to see it. He should've been calling me, begging me to come back, but instead, he was wasting his time with her.

I could feel my jealousy boiling over, the bitterness sharp

and unrelenting. It should have been me in there, not Jean. I was the one who knew how to keep David's attention, not that dull, lifeless girl who wouldn't know how to have a good time if it hit her in the face. I thought about all the nights David and I spent together, the way he'd held me, the way he'd look at me like I was the only thing that mattered. The thought of him sharing that with Jean made me sick. I didn't want to believe it, but the evidence was right in front of me. Jean was trying to take what was mine.

I scrolled through old photos on my phone, pictures of David and me at the lake, pictures from business conferences where I was always his plus one, pictures over elegant dinners, and I felt a pang of longing mixed with fury. We were good together. I'd been happy, and for a while, I thought he had been, too. But now, all I could think about was how to make him realize what he was throwing away. He needed to see that Jean wasn't the answer to anything, that she was just a placeholder, a sad, quiet thing that couldn't give him what he really needed. I'd make him see it. I'd make him remember that I was the best thing that ever happened to him.

As I drove around the block, my mind raced with thoughts of revenge, of how I could make him miss me, make him crawl back to me where he belonged. Jean was nothing but a bump in the road, a temporary distraction. I turned up the radio, letting the music drown out my thoughts as I sped away, determined not to let her win. This wasn't over. Not by a long shot. I'd remind David exactly who I was, and I wouldn't stop until Jean was out of the picture for good.

***

Jean

The rest of the weekend was spent in intense, focused concentration. To my dismay, there was little time for distraction. We ordered delivery—greasy pizza and overly salty Chinese food, the kind that makes your stomach feel heavy but keeps you going. We took turns brewing fresh pots of coffee, the bitter smell permeating the air. After finding the major error, we moved into our largest conference room, attempting to organize everything in the expanse.

On opposite sides of the room, we stretched out on pushed-together padded chairs to snatch a few hours of sleep on Saturday afternoon, our limbs hanging off awkwardly, the cold leather imprinting patterns on our skin. We slept only slightly more on Sunday, the stress driving us back to our laptops and the whiteboards again and again.

Early Monday morning, bleary-eyed and nearly delirious from sleep deprivation, I pulled the last thirty collated pages out of the printer in the copy room, the warm paper sliding into my hands. I stacked them neatly, the sound of rustling sheets cutting through the oppressive quiet. I glanced at the time glowing on the printer's display—4:15 a.m.—and caught movement from the corner of my eye.

David leaned heavily against the doorway, his frame slouched, his usually bright blue eyes dulled by exhaustion. He tried to smile, but it was a weary, fragile thing, and I mirrored it, feeling the weight of the weekend in every muscle and bone.

His shirt was crumpled, his stubble pronounced, and dark circles underscored his eyes like bruises. I imagined I looked just as ragged, my hair a wild mess, my makeup smudged, but at that moment, it didn't matter. We were two people at the end of a marathon, holding ourselves together by sheer willpower.

"Donelson won't be here until two. Will you pitch with me?" His voice was rough, tinged with vulnerability. This afternoon would shape the future of Shep and Son, and I knew how much it meant for him to ask me to stand beside him. But the weight of his request felt almost distant, blunted by the overwhelming need for rest.

I nodded my acceptance, and my words heavy with exhaustion. "I'm going to go get some sleep and a shower."

The thought of returning to the real world felt like surfacing from deep underwater, and a hollow sense of loss settled over me. For the past two days, it had been just the two of us, locked in a bubble of proximity and shared ambitions. Now, we had to rejoin the outside world, and the thought made my shoulders sag as I carried the stack of pages to the conference room. David followed, his footsteps soft behind me.

"How about some breakfast first?" he asked, his voice light but hopeful. He took a bundle of papers from my hands and set them on the oblong table, rubbing his face in a gesture of fatigue.

I hesitated, laying out some more of the copies at each seat, feeling a strange mix of accomplishment and defeat. "I don't think so. I need—"

"—please, Jean. I love you so much." The words tumbled out of him, raw and unguarded.

My head snapped up, my eyes wide as I stared at him. "What did you say?"

He cleared his throat, his face flushing slightly. "I owe you so much."

"Oh, of course." I knew I'd misheard him. I tried to ignore the sudden thudding of my heart, but I couldn't stop the rush of heat that bloomed in my cheeks. I gave in to a yawn, stretching it out until my jaw popped, and waved my hand dismissively. "I need sleep. Rain check on breakfast." I turned away, heading back to his office to gather my coat, shoes, and purse, hoping to hide my rattled nerves.

David quickly caught up. As I snatched my discarded heels

in the corner, he grabbed his own coat and reached for my hand as I turned toward the door. "Come on. I know the perfect place." His grip was gentle but insistent, and the look in his eyes was impossible to refuse.

I sighed, feeling the pull of something unspoken between us. "All right."

"That is, if you'll be seen with me in public. I'm a mess."

"No more than I am," I said, my voice softening as he placed a hand at the small of my back, guiding me out of the office. The touch sent a faint shiver through me, one that I tried to ignore.

"You're always perfect, Jean." His words were barely above a whisper, but they struck something deep, and I found myself blushing, tucking loose strands of red hair behind my ears.

We bundled up, grabbing our boots off the drying rack in the entrance. The winter dawn cold had teeth, and David led the way to his truck as snow crunched under our footsteps. I slid into the leather passenger seat, the frigid material sticking to the backs of my legs as I pulled the door shut with a weary tug. He started the ignition, set the defrost to high, and then scraped the windows.

As we drove through the nearly deserted streets of Elmburn, I let my head rest against the cool glass of the window, the hum of the engine lulling me into a light doze.

The jolt of a turn into a rough parking lot woke me, and I blinked at the sight of a small building with a tin roof and a crooked sign reading JIM'S DINER. A neon display in the window flashed *New Hampshire's Best Coffee, Pancakes, and Grits!* in garish, flickering red. I rubbed my eyes, taking in the scene. As I peered around, I realized we were in Westside, one of Elmburn's rougher neighborhoods and a place I rarely ventured. Across the street, vacant warehouses loomed like silent sentinels, half-swallowed by shadows and snow drifts.

"They serve damn fine breakfast here," David said, his smile easy, as though we were parked outside a five-star bistro instead of a greasy spoon in the sketchiest part of town. He reached over, squeezing my hand lightly, and I let him, the warmth of his touch reassuring.

I stepped out of the truck, eyeing the surroundings warily. The faint glow of streetlights reflected off nearby snowbanks, and a shiver ran up my spine. "We passed a place that has great bagels back toward Northridge," I said, tapping my fingers on the truck's doorframe, ready to retreat.

David laughed. He closed my door and took my elbow gently, guiding me toward the diner. "Not the nicest part of the city, I know, but I come here a lot. It's safe. I promise."

I nodded, allowing him to lead me inside. The diner was a relic from another time, with Marilyn Monroe, Elvis, and

James Dean staring down from faded framed prints and lacquered puzzles on the walls in every possible artistic style. The scent of frying bacon and old coffee lingered in the air.

David pulled me toward a corner booth, the vinyl seats patched with duct tape, and helped me out of my coat. As we sat, "Heartbreak Hotel" dropped on a vintage jukebox in the corner.

"Well, Davey Jones!" A broad-shouldered woman called out, striding out from the kitchen with a swagger. Her gray hair was pulled back into a messy bun, and her eyes twinkled with mischief.

"Morning, Delores," David called back, waving with the kind of familiarity that suggested he was a regular.

Delores grabbed two menus and a pot of coffee, hooking two empty cups on her pinkie. "Do we finally have the pleasure of meeting the fancy fiancée?"

My eyes darted to David, catching a faint blush creeping under his stubble.

"No. This is Jean," he corrected, his voice quiet, but there was an unmistakable pride in how he said my name.

"Oh, sure." Delores set the menus down and poured the coffee pot like it was an extension of herself. "He's told me a lot about you—but he never said his right-hand gal was such a looker!"

I felt my own blush heat my cheeks. "Thank you." I wondered exactly what David had said to her.

"Jean just finished a marathon act of ass-saving," David quipped, his tone playful but sincere.

"Well, good." Delores set a couple of silverware and napkin rolls on the table with a flourish. "I'd hate to think Davey Jones had no one looking out for his fine, sweet ass." She roared with a laugh and headed back to the counter, leaving us in the booth with a wink.

Well, at least I wasn't the only one who was partial to that part of David's anatomy. I sighed and shook my head against the fatigue that let such thoughts run rampant. I was grateful for the distraction of the coffee. I tore the tops off two sugar packets, but David caught my hand before I could reach my cup. The touch was more intimate than I expected, his thumb tracing lazy circles on my skin, and I dropped the packets. The sweet granules scattered.

"I mean it, Jean," he said, refusing to release my hand despite the mess. His voice was low. "I don't know what I'd do without you."

My pulse quickened, and I couldn't help the brief flash of memory—his hand on my hip, his breath warm on the curve of my ear, and the warmth of his chest as I pressed back against him in the employee lounge.

It was an ache I'd buried for so long, and now it felt dangerously close to surfacing. "I…" I tried to pull my hand away, but he held fast, his grip warm and reassuring. "You would have done the same for me."

David shook his head, his gaze unwavering. "You wouldn't have put yourself in this position. I never should've pushed you out of that project in the first place."

His words hung between us, and I found myself staring at the open collar of his shirt, the glimpse of tanned skin beneath. My thoughts spiraled. I forced my gaze up to meet his eyes, but what I saw there—an intensity that mirrored my own longings—made my breath catch.

I opened my mouth to speak, but Delores's sudden approach to take our order made us both jump. I jerked my knee against the table, knocking the coffee cups, and hot liquid spilled across the laminate top and onto our laps. David grabbed napkins from the dispenser, and Delores handed me a rag, laughing at the chaos.

As I dabbed at the coffee on my skirt, David's hand brushed against my bare thigh, lingering just a second too long. The touch sent a spark through me, and I pulled back, stumbling out of the booth.

"I need to—" My eyes darted around, searching for an escape.

Delores pointed past the counter. "Bathroom's down the hall, honey."

Mumbling my thanks, I rushed away, the small bathroom feeling like a sanctuary as I pushed through the door and braced myself against the sink. I stared at my reflection, my hair wild, my eyes wide and glassy. My chest heaved with ragged breaths, and I splashed water on my face, hoping to calm the storm that raged inside me.

"Get a grip," I muttered, my voice echoing off the metal stalls. "You work together. He's your boss." But even as I said it, the words felt hollow. The boundary between us was thinner now, stretched taut by the weekend's long hours and stolen moments. I took a deep breath and steadied myself, resolving to walk out and tell him that we both needed rest, that this was all too much, too soon after Beth.

I turned for the door, but before I could open it, David slipped inside, locking it behind him. The click of the deadbolt was loud in the small space, and my heart skipped a beat.

David looked like a man who had been pulled through hell and hadn't quite made it back. His suit, once sharp and tailored, now hung on him like a secondhand mistake—wrinkled, stained, and barely hanging onto any sense of professionalism. His white shirt was unbuttoned at the collar, revealing a glimpse of skin that was as tense and weary as the rest of him. His hair over the weekend had become a tousled mess of blonde that seemed to do whatever it damn well pleased, and I found myself wondering if that's how it would greet me the morning-after too. There was something infuriatingly magnetic about him, like a storm you couldn't quite bring yourself to outrun.

The record in the jukebox moved on to "All Shook Up."

*Damn right I was.* "What are you—"

"Just let me say this." His voice was urgent, and he stepped closer to me. I leaned back against the sink, feeling the cool porcelain press into my back.

His eyes unsettled me the most—piercing blue that cut through the mess like the one thing he hadn't lost control of. They were sharp, assessing, and just a little too intense, as always. In his most disheveled state, he exuded a kind of reckless charm, like he was one bad decision away from either saving the day or burning the whole place down.

"Jean, I've known you for years, but I don't think I ever really *saw* you."

I looked away, my throat tightening. "Please, David. Not now."

"Why not? It's never the right time for this kind of thing." His voice was low, pleading. "I think we might feel the same—"

"The *same*?" My voice wavered, a tremor of anger and hurt.

"The same fleeting feelings you've discovered over one weekend? Or the same feelings I've been burying for the past six years?" My fists clenched at my sides, the words spilling out like a dam breaking. *How dare he? Now, after all this time. AFTER Beth.* "Or maybe the same heartbreak I've felt planning your engagement party. To *my* step-sister." I shoved a hand against his chest, pushing him back. "I'm so tired of—"

David's lips crashed against mine, cutting off my words, the kiss fierce and desperate. I pulled away, gasping, but he followed, kissing me again, softer this time, his mouth coaxing rather than demanding. His hands gripped my waist, drawing me close, and I sighed against his lips, the fight leaving me in a rush.

"David," I whispered, my voice shaky.

"I know," he murmured, his breath warm against my ear. He kissed along my jaw, the rough scrape of his stubble sending shivers down my spine. My hands roamed over his chest, up to his neck, tangling in his hair. The weekend's intimacy, our shared exhaustion, and the unspoken tension that had built between us made me reckless, and I let myself sink into the moment, savoring the feel of him, the taste of him.

But even as we kissed, doubts simmered in the back of my mind. Was this just the release of pent-up tension, or something real? I shifted, and my snow boots slipped on the slick bathroom tile. David steadied me, and our eyes met, a silent question hanging between us.

A wiggle of the door made us both jump. It was followed by a sharp knock. "Hello! Why is this door locked?" A woman's voice—impatient, annoyed.

David caught my hand as I reached for the lock and kissed me one last time, quick and urgent. I unlocked and pulled the door open, and we stumbled out, flushed and disheveled. An elderly woman with blue hair glared at us, her eyes narrowing as we hurried past.

I snatched my coat and purse from the booth, my thoughts muddled, my body humming with exhaustion and adrenaline. "I need to go home and get some rest," I said, my voice hollow.

David nodded, throwing cash on the table for the coffee. We walked outside into the gray light of early morning, cold clinging to the streets. As we climbed into his truck, the familiar sounds—the creak of the leather seats, the click of the seatbelts—felt unbearably loud, the silence between us heavy and charged.

As David drove toward the Shep and Son parking lot, I fiddled with the magnetic clasp on my purse, my thoughts a tangled mess. I pulled out my phone, the screen lighting up with a flurry of notifications. I scrolled through them absently, my mind barely processing the messages. As I set the phone on the center console, my fingers brushed against his hand on the gearshift.

I shied away, sinking back into the seat, my head heavy with fatigue. David glanced at me, his expression unreadable, and I forced myself to meet his eyes.

"I don't want to just be your rebound," I said quietly, the words slipping out before I could stop them.

David's jaw tightened, and he nodded slowly. "You're not a rebound, Jean. Things with Beth had been off the rails for a long time."

"But you asked her to marry you." My voice was a whisper, the weight of everything between us pressing down like a lead blanket. I fiddled with the hem of my coat, my thoughts drifting back to the day Beth had flaunted her engagement ring at the office, the smug smile on her lips as she twirled it in the light. I'd gone home sick that day, drinking myself into oblivion to numb the sting.

David reached out, his hand brushing mine. "I just... I don't know. I went along with it. It seemed like the right thing to do at the time. My dad... he'd wanted me to settle down. One of the last things he said before his stroke was that he hoped to see me married."

"But do you love her?"

He hesitated, his brow furrowing. "I loved the idea of her,

of what we were supposed to be. But she's not the person I thought she was. She's… different when no one's watching."

I gave a short bitter laugh in response. Didn't I know it? I traced the smooth curve of the window frame, my mind swirling with memories of Beth's cruelty, the ways she'd twisted people around her finger, even as a kid. I wondered if David saw through her now, the way I always had, or if he was still clinging to the image he'd built up in his head.

But what about me? Hadn't I been hiding, too? Six years of quiet longing, six years of keeping my feelings locked away while playing the part of the professional. Was I any less guilty of pretending? My eyes felt heavy, my vision blurring as I stared out at the streets passing by. Fatigue wrapped around me like a thick fog, clouding my thoughts.

David pulled into the Shep and Son parking lot, his truck idling beside mine. He got out with me. I started the ignition and he used his brush to attack the powered snow that had accumulated over the weekend. As I scraped a bottom layer of ice off the front window, I glanced at him. There was a hardness about him, an unspoken weariness that clung to him like a shadow. David Shep was a man who carried his battles visibly—on his clothes, in the tight line of his jaw, and especially in the way those blue eyes watched the world like it had already disappointed him a hundred times over.

41

"Get some rest," he said gently as we finish with the snow and ice. "We'll figure this out."

I nodded, his fingers brushed my hand, but I was too tired to say anything else. I climbed into my car and watched as David's truck pulled away. Only when his taillights disappeared did I realize what I'd forgotten—my phone, still sitting on the center console of his truck, left behind in the muddled haze of everything we'd been through.

I sighed, rubbing my temples. I'd have to deal with it later. Right now, all I wanted was to crawl into bed and shut out the world. I turned up the volume on the radio. The oldies station I listened to was playing Elvis's "Too Much."

"Of course," I muttered, taking it was a warning, as I pulled out of the snowy parking lot and headed for home.

# Chapter Two

*David*

Even though I'd napped for six hours, the fatigue clung to me like a second skin, and I dozed off again, my forehead pressed against the hot, wet tiles of the shower wall. The drumming of water and rising steam blurred my thoughts, a soothing static that washed away the sharp edges of reality.

I woke with a start when the water turned cold, a frigid jolt that pulled me back to the present. I turned off the shower and stumbled out, grabbing my towel from the hook. The fabric was rough against my skin, scraping away the remnants of sleep as I dried off. I could still feel the weight of exhaustion, not just in my body, but somewhere deeper, pressing down on my spirit like a heavy stone.

"Yoo-hoo!" came a voice, syrupy sweet and nauseatingly familiar. *Beth. What the hell was she doing here?*

My spine stiffened as I wrapped the towel around my waist. The last thing I needed was her theatrics. I stalked out of the bathroom to find her lounging on my bed like a queen in court, propped up against my pillows with her high heels still on, ankles crossed. She was wearing a tight cream-colored sleeveless dress that hit just above her knees. She drew a manicured fingernail—a shade of red too perfect, too sharp—across her calf, her movements slow and deliberate. It was a taunt, a challenge, a game she knew all too well how to play.

I shot her an annoyed look that I hope conveyed disgust as well. "After our last conversation, I don't know how you have the gall to be here."

Beth raised her hands, palms up, her smile unwavering. It was the kind of expression that promised nothing but trouble from her. "If you would have just answered your phone, I wouldn't have had to walk in on you." Her voice dripped with faux innocence, each word laced with hidden barbs.

I hadn't charged my phone since before the diner that morning; a small, stupid oversight, but one that now felt monumental. "Why are you here?" I demanded, frustration giving a sharpened edge to my voice.

"Is Jean here?" Beth's gaze flicked past me, scanning the bathroom doorway like she expected Jean to appear any second, a ghost conjured by her suspicion.

"No," I snapped, feeling my temper flare. "Why would she be?"

Beth's expression twisted into a smirk, her eyes bright with mischief. "Well, her phone is out on your table. She must be around here somewhere." She tilted her chin, eyes wide with mock surprise.

I clenched my jaw. "Not that it's any of your business, but she forgot her phone in my truck. I was charging it for her."

"You've been working some long nights together." She said it with observation, and I could see the jealousy she was trying to hide.

I wasn't going to the baited. I was at least smart enough to know that Beth would be the last person Jean would want me to discuss anything with. "We're through, Beth. Give me back my keys. I'll get yours." I headed for the kitchen where I kept them.

A loud buzz sounded—the call button for the front entrance. Jean's voice crackled through, strained and anxious. "Hello? David?"

Beth was closer than I was to the wall panel next to the bed's headboard. Her eyes flashed with malice. She lunged for it, her movements swift and serpentine, pressing the button before I could stop her. "Sorry, Jeanie, he's not decent at the moment," she crooned into the intercom, her voice dripping with lust.

"Beth?" Jean's response tinged with disbelief, the kind of hurt that cut deeper than any insult.

I elbowed Beth away from the panel, my patience worn thin. "Sorry, Jean. She was just leaving. What's up?"

Beth languished on the bed, grinning.

There was a pause, heavy and awkward, before Jean's guarded reply filtered through. "I forgot my phone in your truck, and I wanted to make sure you made it to the Donelson pitch."

"Come up." I pressed the entrance unlock, my finger lingering on the button as if the connection would somehow erase the mess unfolding in my apartment.

Beth's posture was relaxed, yet her tone was anything but. "Poor David. You're going to need a shoulder to cry on, so it's too bad that I'm persona non grata—at the moment."

I shot her a cold glare. "Say whatever you came to say and get out."

She dragged her nails along the bedsheet, like a cat stretching, a slow, sensuous movement that set my nerves on edge, and then she stood from my bed. Without warning, she began to unbutton her dress, each flick of her fingers a deliberate provocation.

"Knock it off," I ordered, my voice stern and low.

The sound of the elevator ding echoed through my flat,

followed by soft, hesitant footsteps of Jean approaching the foyer. Beth unhooked the front clasp of her pink lace bra, her eyes never leaving mine, relishing every second of my discomfort.

"Oh, by the way," she said, tossing the words over her shoulder as she turned toward my bedroom door, "your father died this morning."

The ground shifted beneath me, my grip on reality slipping. I grabbed her elbow, yanking her back into my room, my voice a rough whisper. "You're lying." It felt like an attack, another one of her cruel games. Dad's death was possible, expected even, but coming from Beth's mouth, it felt like a weapon.

She met my gaze, her expression shifting—just for a moment—from smug satisfaction to something that looked like compassion. It was gone as quickly as it appeared, replaced by her usual icy detachment. "No, I'm not. The hospice facility tried contacting you. When they couldn't reach you, they called me." She took a step back, her composure cracking slightly. "Apparently, you forgot to update the alternative contact number for flavor-of-the-week." Her voice turned venomous, her words digging deeper than they should have.

Shock rolled through me, numbing my senses. For a split second, I let my guard down, and Beth seized the opportunity, yanking the towel from my waist with a quick, deft motion. She

47

blew an air kiss as she tossed my towel back toward the bathroom, just as Jean appeared in the doorway.

She froze, her eyes wide, her gaze darting between Beth, now fastening her bra and re-buttoning her dress and me, naked and exposed, still dripping from the shower. The disbelief on her face was palpable, a raw wound laid bare. I felt stripped not just of my dignity, but of every ounce of control I'd fought to maintain.

Beth shoved past Jean, her hips swaying with each click of her heels against the tile. "Really, David! This can't happen again." She threw a final glance over her shoulder. "Take your keys back!" I heard the metal ring clatter and slide across a countertop.

Jean's face fell, her mouth opening as if to speak, but no words came. The weight of the moment pressed down on us, heavy and suffocating. My head spun, and I reached back, gripping the bureau against the wall to steady myself. My pulse pounded in my ears, each beat a reminder of the chaos Beth had unleashed.

Jean took a hesitant step forward, concern etched into the lines of her face. "David, you're white as a sheet. What—" She reached out, catching my elbow when I started to lose my balance. "Why don't you sit down?" Her voice was gentle, but I could hear the strain beneath it.

I sank onto my bed. She moved away briefly, retrieving the towel Beth had tossed away, and draped it over my lap with a quiet, unspoken kindness that twisted my insides.

"What's wrong?" she asked, her voice soft, yet probing.

"Beth said..." My throat tightened, the words catching. "My phone. I need my phone."

Jean searched quickly, finding it in the pocket of my discarded pants on the floor. She powered it on, but the screen blazed for only a couple of seconds before a low battery warning flashed. Then it went black. She fished the charging cord off the floor next to my bedside table and plugged it in, crossing her arms and staring at the phone as if willing it to charge faster, her brow furrowed in concentration.

I leaned forward, resting my head in my hands, the towel beneath my elbows. My mind raced. Beth had made it look like I'd hooked up with her—like I was weak, fickle, untrustworthy. Hours ago, I had told Jean that she wasn't a rebound. Now, all of that was in jeopardy. I felt like the biggest fool in the world.

"I didn't..." The words came out stilted, half-formed. I'd meant to explain what happened, how Beth had shown up uninvited, how she was only trying to make me look bad, how she had completely succeeded. But none of that connected with my speech ability. Instead, I said, "Dad's dead."

Jean's reaction was immediate; she moved closer, sitting

down on the mattress next to me, wrapping her arms around my shoulders, pulling me into her. I buried my face against the soft fabric of her blouse. She was warm, solid, a lifeline of which I was in desperate need.

"I'm so sorry, David."

"Beth's number," I muttered against her shoulder, fighting back the tide of emotions threatening to drown me.

"Of course," she murmured, rubbing my back with a slow, soothing rhythm. "Your phone was dead, so they called her as an alternate contact." She pulled back, her hands still on my shoulders, grounding me. "You don't have to explain."

"Yes, I do." I clenched my jaw, the anger bubbling up. "Beth—"

Jean cut me off, her concern giving way to practicality. "Have you eaten anything yet today?"

I shook my head, still dazed.

She got up and moved out of the room with quiet efficiency. A few minutes later, she returned with a plate of toast and a glass of water. "You need to eat."

I picked up a toast triangle, holding it between my fingers like a foreign object. I didn't want food. I wanted to undo the last fifteen minutes, to go back to the part where I still had a shred of control over my life. But I took a bite anyway, the dry crunch echoing in my ears. Jean was watching me, her expression soft as if she could sense the storm raging inside me.

"The Donelson pitch," I mumbled around the toast, glancing at the clock on the wall. "His flight's landing soon. I can't cancel."

"Don't worry about it," Jean said firmly. "I'll handle him. Eat."

I watched her and felt myself torn between gratitude and shame. Beth had twisted the knife deep, but Jean was still here, still holding me together. I took a deep breath, feeling the weight of her faith in me. Or was I fooling myself? Was it her job that she was more concerned about at this point? She knew how much leveraged on a success with Donelson.

She stood, leaning toward the bureau and set the plate and glass down on top. She took another triangle and toast and handed it to me. I dropped it on the bed and pulled her against me, gathering her into my arms.

She responded with a slight, "oof," off-balance, but she hugged me back immediately.

I took a deep breath with my face buried in her neck, reveling in the softness of her hair. She smelled like amber and ginger mixed with a brief but sharp citrus. The scent was completely fitting for Jean and a balm to my nerves. "I absolutely did not invite Beth over here to—"

"—I know," she said quickly. "She was trying to hurt you.

51

That's the way she controls things. Just enough hurt, then just enough love, and then you're hers to hurt in all the ways she wants. It's how she's always done things."

I released a frustrated sigh against the curve of her neck.

"Hey." She leaned her head back slightly, looking into my eyes and laying a gentle hand along my cheek. Her thumb skimmed my jawline. "Don't let her get to you."

I felt completely lost. The only thing I was sure about was that I wanted to press Jean onto the bed and piledrive her into the mattress until every other thought fled and nothing else mattered. Thank God I was with it enough to know that as amazing as it might be, it was the definition of a poor coping mechanism.

"I don't know what to do, Jean."

She smiled at me. "First, you eat." She picked up the discarded piece of toast from the comforter and popped the corner in my mouth. I caught the edge and bit down.

"Then," Jean moved off my lap and snatched my charging phone. "You call hospice and tell them you'll be over soon." She pressed the power button and the screen lit up. She finagled the charging cord from its tangle around the bedside lamp and handed the phone to me.

"I plugged your phone in on the table in the dining room," I told Jean. She walked out of the room to retrieve it, and I pressed recall on one of the six missed calls from the hospice facility.

"Good afternoon. Shady Elm." The receptionist's voice was much too cheerful.

"This is David Shep. My—"

"Oh, Mr. Shep! We've been trying to locate you. I'm so sorry to inform you that your father passed away this morning."

My stomach dropped to hear the words from a source other than Beth. "I've already been informed."

"Did Ms. Oakley find you then? We tried all your contact—"

"—Yes, she found me." I couldn't keep the curtness from my voice. "What do I need to do?"

Jean sat back down on the bed and squeezed my free hand.

"Please come here as soon as possible," the receptionist said. "We'll need you to identify and release your father."

*Identify him.* The last two months I could barely identify him—nor he, me. His entire life and career had been about the use of his brain, and in the end, it was cruelly taken from him.

"Mr. Shep? Are you there?" the receptionist asked.

"Yes," I said, clearing my throat. "I'll be there in a half hour."

"Thank you, Mr. Shep. See you soon." The line beeped as the connection ended. I tossed my phone toward my pillow, and

Jean handed me the glass of water from the bureau.

"I have to go 'identify and release' Dad." An involuntary shiver ran through me as I sipped.

"Do you want me to talk to Donelson? Maybe I can push the meeting to a dinner. Then I could help you now and meet with him later."

"No. He won't like that. I can manage this, I think."

Jean laid her cheek against my shoulder, rubbing my back. "Of course you can."

"Later, though, the whole funeral thing. I might need some help. Hospice helped me set up a few things after the doctor said it was only a matter of time, but…" My mind was so hazy that I couldn't express myself clearly.

"Sure. Whatever you need." The warmth of her smile helped to melt some of the ice gathering in my gut. "I'd like to help for his sake, too. I was always fond of Edgar. He taught me so much."

I nodded. "He thought a lot of you, too." I gave a short laugh. "There were days at work where I'm pretty sure he wished you were his blood relation—not me."

Jean leaned against me, and I held her. "He loved you, David. He just didn't know how to show it. I think he was hard on you because of it." She pulled away. "Are you sure you'll be okay on your own?"

I nodded.

She glanced at the clock. Donelson would be at the office in less than an hour. She stood up. "I don't think you should drive yourself."

I stood, too, wrapping the towel around my hips.

"I could drop you off," she offered.

"I'll just grab a cab."

She rifled a hand through her beautiful red hair, and I couldn't stand it. I slipped my hands around her waist and pulled her close. Jean's lips were soft and full, like an escape into the fluffy clouds of a pale pink sunset, gentle and warm, a fleeting taste of something I'd craved for longer than I'd ever dared to admit. As we kissed, the world around us seemed to dissolve into a hazy blur of heat and want, every worry, every lingering doubt fading into nothingness. She leaned into me, her body pressing closer, and I felt her surrender in the way her breath hitched and her fingers curled around my upper arms, pulling me in like I was the only thing holding her steady. I could taste her on my lips, the subtle hint of coffee mingling with toothpaste. It was intoxicating—the sweet, soft heat of her mouth, the way she responded so wholeheartedly, like this kiss was a promise neither of us had ever spoken aloud but had been silently yearning to fulfill.

My pulse quickened and my senses honed in on the

singular, undeniable truth: I wanted her, not just in this stolen moment but in every small, quiet second that came after.

She moved against me, her hands sliding up to cup my face, her touch feather-light but commanding, and I let myself fall deeper, caught up in the way she kissed me back with a fierce, unrestrained tenderness that stole the breath from my lungs. Her lips were warm and searching, exploring the space between us with a soft, languid urgency that spoke of all the things we'd never said. I wanted to memorize every detail—the slight tremble of her lower lip, the way she sighed against me when our mouths met, the intoxicating blend of nervous energy and raw, unguarded desire that flowed between us.

It was a kiss that tasted of everything we'd been through—years of friendship, quiet longing, unspoken fears, and the fragile, delicate hope that maybe this time, we could rewrite our story. As we pulled apart, I rested my forehead gently against hers, and I knew this wasn't just about the kiss; it was about what it meant.

It was about every stolen glance, every lingering touch, every late-night conversation where we danced around the truth. Jean was my calm in the storm, my unexpected escape, and with her lips still tingling against mine, I felt something I hadn't in a long time—like I was finally home.

"Jean, it wasn't just this weekend. I've felt close to you for a long time, but I was worried…" *What?* What had honestly been so important that I hadn't made this amazing woman a bigger part of my life? My head was spinning, and every thought that came to mind seemed trivial.

She nodded her head and laid a hand against my chest, silent for a few moments as if fighting her own internal struggle. "I'll let you know how Donelson goes," she said it quietly and stepped back out of my arms.

"Thanks."

"Like I said, whatever you need. Don't be afraid to ask." She gave a brief wave from the doorway and her footsteps with softer heels than Beth's—or maybe it was just her stride—moved toward the foyer and the elevator beyond.

I sat back down on the bed and rested my elbows on my knees, my head in my hands. I pressed my palms against wet eyes until I saw shaking bursts of light and then moved to get dressed.

\*\*\*

*Jean*

The heavy oak doors of Shep and Son's most luxurious conference room shut behind me with a soft click, and I took a deep breath, the weight of the moment settling on my shoulders. Sunlight streamed through the tall windows, illuminating the polished oak table and casting golden streaks across the floor. I was reminded of the Dickinson poem on the wall in my office—that winter afternoon shaft of light. It could illuminate so much that was hidden, so much we needed, but wouldn't know until it was too late. I prayed I wasn't too late to win the boost Shep and Son sorely needed.

I smoothed down my pencil skirt and adjusted the collar of my blouse, every detail meticulously planned to convey confidence and control. The next hour could change everything for us.

The room was filled with the quiet buzz of conversation as Frederick Donelson's team settled into their seats. Frederick himself sat at the far end of the table, his presence commanding without effort. He wasn't what I'd expected—there was nothing of the typical eccentric billionaire about him. No arrogance, no pretension. Instead, there was a sense of authenticity, a man who had lived many lives and learned the hard way what truly mattered.

He was older than me by at least fifteen years, with a cleanly shaven face and head that gave him a notable look and sharp brown eyes that missed nothing. He wore an impeccably tailored suit, yet somehow seemed comfortable, as if the clothes didn't stretch taut over a muscular build that one would expect on a man two decades younger.

The curve of a tribal tattoo snaked up the side of his neck and ended behind his right ear. That, too, would have been expected of someone much younger. I knew, however, that the ink had been applied by an ancient method during the six months he lived with a primitive tribe in Tanzania. The adventures he'd experienced there made up only a small portion of the fantastic life we'd hopefully be expounding on in his books.

He leaned back in his chair, fingers steepled, watching me with an intensity that would have unnerved most people. But I felt steady and ready, in my element. Adrenaline was quickly shoving aside the sleep debt that would no doubt plague me for weeks.

To Donelson's right sat Jake Ross, his agent, a man known for his cutthroat negotiation skills and a reputation for keeping the Frederick Donelson empire running smoothly. Across from him were two lawyers, one scribbling notes while the other tapped away on his laptop. They all exuded power, wealth, and a sense of self-assuredness, but none more so than Frederick himself.

"Jean Price," Donelson said before I could introduce myself.

"That's right, Mr. Donelson." I walked over to shake his hand.

He stood. "I hear remarkable things about you from your competitors." His hand was warm, dry, and covered mine like a lion's mitt enveloping a kitten's paw.

I was surprised. "Is that so?"

He nodded and introduced Jake and the lawyers.

"It's a pleasure to meet you," I said. "Unfortunately, our acting manager and commissioning editor, David Shep, can't join us today."

"Yes, our condolences," Donelson said with sincerity. "We heard about his father. I have enjoyed the phone conversations with David over the past couple of months, but I'm more excited to see what you have for us today."

"Jean," Jake said, nodding to me. "Whenever you're ready."

I clicked the remote, and the lights dimmed as the first slide of our presentation appeared on the screen ahead of us. Donelson sat back down, and I strode to the front of the room. He, surprisingly, gave me a small, encouraging smile, and I launched into the pitch.

"Gentlemen, today I'm going to show you how Shep and Son can help Donelson Enterprises redefine your brand's narrative, not just in the market but in the hearts of your audience. What we're proposing isn't just a literary campaign— it's a movement."

I clicked through the slides, weaving together a story of innovation, community engagement, and strategic positioning that would set Donelson Enterprises apart from every competitor. Each slide built on the last, detailing the concept that felt like it was months in the refining process, even though we'd finished it only hours ago. David's big-picture ideas and my meticulous execution merged into something powerful, something uniquely ours.

Donelson listened intently, his gaze flicking every now and then to the slides, but unusually glued to me. It should have made me nervous, but it only served to make me bolder. As I spoke, I could feel the energy shift in the room. The lawyers stopped typing, Jake leaned forward, and Frederick's eyes sparkled with something between intrigue and approval. I talked about leveraging digital platforms in new ways, about turning everyday customers into loyal brand advocates. Every word was crafted to connect with what I knew mattered most to Frederick Donelson— impact, legacy, and human stories.

When I reached the slide that outlined the personal touches—the community initiatives, the charity partnerships, the storytelling campaigns—I saw Frederick's posture change. He leaned forward, elbows on the table, absorbing every word as if he were already imagining how it would look, how it would feel.

"This isn't just about selling books," I said, pausing to meet his gaze directly. "It's about creating connections. It's about making your brand synonymous with hope, progress, and real change in people's lives. We can do that together."

Frederick's expression softened, and for a brief moment, I saw a flicker of something deeper—pain, maybe, or memories that hadn't faded as much as he'd like. I knew a little about his past, about the daughter he'd lost by suicide, and I'd woven that understanding into every part of this pitch without ever making it obvious. It wasn't manipulation—it was empathy, and it mattered.

The final slide appeared, and I wrapped up with a clear, concise outline of the next steps. "We believe in this vision, Mr. Donelson. It already exists in you and your experiences. At Shep and Son, we know we're the right partner to uncover it fully and polish it until it shines. Let's make it happen."

The room was silent for a moment after I finished, the kind of silence that hangs in the air when something important has just transpired. Donelson was the first to break it, clapping slowly and deliberately. Jake and the lawyers quickly joined in, but it was the primary approval that sent a surge of relief and pride through me.

"That was impressive, Jean," Donelson said, his voice smooth and sincere. "You've captured exactly what we're aiming for—and, frankly, more than I'd dared to hope for."

"Thank you, Mr. Donelson," I replied, trying to keep the smile on my face from looking too triumphant. "I've put my heart into this because I believe in your brand and what it stands for."

He gave a small, knowing nod. "You've done more than that. You've captured a vision. And that's rare. You had better call me Frederick."

He turned to his team, his tone shifting from the thoughtful entrepreneur to the decisive leader. "Jake, review all the documents with the team. I want this signed and sealed today."

Jake nodded, immediately digging into the stack of documents in front of him. The lawyers exchanged quick glances, and one of them began typing furiously. There was a flurry of movement around him, but Frederick remained calm, watching me with an appraising look.

He leaned back in his chair, and I thought for a second that this was it—that we'd done it, and that all the hard work had paid off. But then he surprised me.

"Jean," he said, his voice softer now, almost playful, "you've impressed me, and I'm not easily impressed these days. But I have one more question before we finalize things."

"Of course," I said, masking my sudden apprehension. "What would you like to know?"

"What's the best restaurant in Elmburn?"

The question caught me off guard. I'd been prepared to discuss metrics, branding strategies, and market demographics—but not the finer points of local dining. Still, I recovered quickly, thinking of the place I always went when I needed to celebrate or escape for a quiet evening.

"Amelie's," I said, smiling at the thought. "It's a small, intimate spot with amazing food. The chef is French, and she only uses seasonal ingredients, so the menu changes constantly."

"Amelie's," Frederick repeated. "Sounds perfect. I'm taking you there tonight, Jean. And I won't take no for an answer."

I blinked, caught off guard again, but this time by the unexpected invitation. There was no mistaking his intent—he was interested, and not just in the pitch. A quick glance at Jake showed that even the unflappable agent was momentarily thrown. I hesitated, the professional in me warning that this might blur lines. But Frederick's expression was so genuine, so entirely without pretense, that I found myself nodding before I could overthink it.

"I'd be honored," I said, and I meant it. Frederick's smile widened, and he looked almost boyish, as if he'd just scored a small victory of his own.

"Excellent," he said, rising from his chair and buttoning his suit jacket. "I'll have my driver pick you up at seven."

With that, he shook my hand—another confident, enveloping grip that lingered just a second longer than strictly necessary—and walked out of the room, his entourage following close behind. I watched him go, my mind still reeling from the pitch's success and the surprising turn of events.

As the door closed behind them, I took a moment to absorb what had just happened. The deal was in the bag, and Frederick Donelson had not only seen value in my ideas but also in me. It was a heady feeling, a mix of professional triumph and the electric twinge of something personal just beginning to take shape.

I packed up my materials slowly, savoring the moment of quiet victory. Whatever came next, I knew that today was a turning point. I'd stepped out of the shadows and into my own light, showing the world what I was truly capable of.

The far entrance cracked open and three heads popped into view. Jerry, Grace, and Steve looked questioningly at me. I couldn't hide the huge smile on my face. Grace raced in first, squealing with the delight I felt. Hugs and high-fives were exchanged all around, and everyone talked over the other.

My face hurt from smiling. Tonight, I'd celebrate. But tomorrow, the real work would begin. I felt ready for whatever came next.

***

*David*

My phone buzzed in my pocket as I walked down the ramp away from the hospice facility, the chill of the approaching evening seeping into my bones. I felt drained, like the life had been wrung out of me along with the endless paperwork and forced conversations with strangers who spoke in careful, rehearsed tones.

Identifying Dad's body had been a gut punch I hadn't been prepared for—the man who had loomed so large in my life reduced to a cold, lifeless figure on the bleached white linens of the patient bed. I had spent too long staring at him, searching for something familiar in his face, but it was gone. There was only a shell, and the realization twisted my insides.

I stopped, knees wobbling beneath me, and leaned against the handrail for support. The cold metal stung against my palms, the pain a small anchor to reality. I pulled out my phone, half expecting bad news, half dreading what I might find. Relief washed over me when I saw Jean's name in the notification.

*DONELSON HUGE SUCCESS!* she'd texted. *He can't wait to work with us! He's insisting on a dinner.*

I managed a faint smile, despite the ache still clawing at my

66

chest. Jean had pulled it off—of course she had—and in that moment, it felt like a much-needed win. I typed back quickly, fingers moving on autopilot.

*Huge relief! You can go if you want. I need sleep. THANK YOU. I don't know what I'd do without you.*

The phone buzzed almost immediately with her reply.

*Ok. Need anything? How did the hospice visit go?*

My mind flashed back to the room, the sterile smell of antiseptic mingling with the metallic tang of dread.

*Not what I expected. Meeting for funeral arrangements tomorrow at 11. Will you come with me?* I asked, surprised by how anxious I felt waiting for her reply.

*Definitely. Want to meet or pick up?* Jean was the steady hand on my shoulder when everything else felt like it was spinning out of control and not just at work. The day-to-day grind, employee issues, relationships, problems with Beth the last year, even the damned engagement party. How had I not seen that?

I pushed myself off the railing, forcing my legs to move, and texted back as I made my way to the sidewalk to wait for my approaching ride share. The packed snow on the roads gleamed under streetlights that flickered on.

*Come stay with me tonight after Donelson dinner?* I typed, feeling a surge of hope. The text bubbles floated, then disappeared. Floated, then stopped. The silence of the winter evening pressed in as I waited. My phone buzzed just as I unlocked the door.

*Think I need a little time. Send the address for funeral home. Meet you there at 11.*

I stared at the screen, re-reading Jean's lukewarm response that left my stomach churning with a bitter mix of guilt and dread. Something was off—her words were too flat, too distant, lacking the usual spark that always made me feel like she was on my side. Had Beth's charade this morning been too much? Did Jean believe what she saw or what I told her? Had this new connection been twisted into something that was destined to fail?

And then there was the Donelson project, my latest screw-up hanging over me like a lead weight. I'd procrastinated, gotten lost in distractions, and left Jean to pick up my slack. She'd carried the project through the weekend when it should've been me leading, and now I couldn't help but wonder if she'd finally seen through me—the expensive suit, the practiced charm, all the trappings my father had always criticized as empty posturing. Maybe Jean was realizing what I'd been afraid of all along: that I'm just another disappointment, unworthy of the support she'd given me, and far too close to becoming exactly what everyone else had already written me off as.

My ride share pulled up, and I sat down on the cold leather of the back seat and stared at my phone. I navigated to the funeral home website, copying the address into a reply before adding a bland response, *OK, see you then.* I hit send and tucked the phone away in my coat pocket. The knot in my stomach didn't ease.

The ride home was a blur of taillights and street signs, my mind churning over Jean's response. Was it hesitation? Doubt? I knew this weekend had been a mess, but I had hoped we were in it together, navigating the chaos side by side. I checked my phone at every stoplight, hoping for a follow-up, an explanation, anything, but there was nothing. My thoughts circled back to Beth, to the way she had twisted the knife, making everything seem so much worse than it was. I could almost hear her laugh, like she'd planned it all.

I was so lost in thought that I nearly walked straight into the person waiting in front of the elevator in my parking garage. My eyes snapped up at the last second.

"Watch it, tiger."

*Beth.* She looked immaculate, like always, her dark hair perfectly styled, lips painted with that shade of red that once made my pulse quicken. Now, it just made me nervous.

I gritted my teeth, trying to rein in my frustration with her and waited for her to give some explanation for her unwanted presence.

Beth's smile was sharp, predatory almost. She reached out, her fingers grazing the sleeve of my coat, and I jerked back. Her pout was almost convincing, a practiced expression she'd perfected over years of manipulation. "Don't be like that. I just want to help."

I stabbed the elevator call button with more force than necessary. "I don't need your help."

She tilted her head, her eyes narrowing with calculated concern. "Is Jeanie coming?"

I jangled my keys in my pocket, each clink a jarring reminder of the day's frustrations. "She's meeting me tomorrow."

Beth let out a low whistle, her eyes flicking to my neck. "That vein's popping out." She reached a finger toward the spot, and I shifted away, recoiling from her touch. "Is she going cold on you all of a sudden?"

I clenched my fists. "We've had a long weekend."

Beth's expression softened, and for the first time in months, her voice lost its edge. "I'm sorry." The words hung in the air, awkward and out of place.

I shot her a skeptical glance. "For what?"

"About your father. And about the way it ended between

us." She hesitated, as if weighing how much to reveal. "I take most of the credit for that."

The elevator doors slid open, and I stepped inside, my back stiff, my gaze fixed on the glowing numbers. I pressed the close door button.

She took an easy step forward, placing her hand against the doorframe, stopping the action.

"Is there something else?"

She leaned against the frame, her posture almost meek. "Please, David," she said, her voice softening further. "Let me help you somehow. Maybe I could make you dinner. You're looking a little pale."

I could feel my resolve crumbling, the edges of my anger blurring under the weight of everything. I'd spent over a year with Beth—longer than I had with any woman before, and yet, not well enough to see our downfall coming. She was right. She had ended it, not me. But part of me still felt the loss, the sting of being discarded. Maybe it was pride. Maybe it was loneliness. Or maybe it was the simple, human need to not be alone, even if it was just for a meal.

I hesitated, a war raging inside. The logical side screamed to push her away, to keep her at arm's length, but there was another part, quieter, more desperate, that wanted to say yes. Just for tonight. Just to feel something familiar.

My thoughts flicked back to Jean's text. *Think I need a little time.* I felt completely and utterly alone.

"Truce?" Beth asked, stepping inside the elevator, her eyes wide, almost pleading. "Just dinner, David. That's it."

I stared at her, trying to reconcile the person in front of me with the woman who had torn my life apart. There was no heat left between us, no flicker of the old spark, but the history lingered, heavy and unavoidable. "Something to eat. That's it," I said finally, my voice flat, tired.

Beth nodded, her smile small, tentative. "Thank you, David. I feel awful about what happened between us."

I clenched my jaw, swallowing the bitterness. "No tricks." I pressed the button for the 32nd floor.

"Of course," she promised, though her eyes gave away nothing as the doors finally closed.

Beth stood beside me, quiet, uncharacteristically subdued, and I found myself wondering—not for the first time—what her endgame was. But for now, I was too tired to care.

# Chapter Three

*Jean*

I arrived at Amelie's fifteen minutes early, nerves fluttering in my stomach like fireflies to the night. The restaurant, tucked away in a quiet corner of Elmburn, had always been my secret escape—a place where I could sip wine, enjoy an amazing meal, and let the world fall away. Tonight, though, it felt different.

Just as I was about to open the car door, my phone rang, the sharp sound startling me. My heart leapt, hoping it was David, but it wasn't. I sagged back against the driver's seat, disappointment sinking into my bones. My news that the meeting with Frederick Donelson and his team was a success garnered only a thumbs-up emoji. I'd waited patiently, thinking he might have still been finishing up at the hospice facility or maybe even meeting with the funeral home. But it was now almost 7 o'clock, and still, there was no additional response.

My brother George's goofy smile filled the screen. I swiped to answer, setting the phone up against the steering wheel for the video call. "Hi, George."

"Auntie Jean!" Mary's excited voice rang out in the background, her youthful exuberance infectious even over the phone. She eked into the picture from the corner.

"Hey, Mary!" I forced a smile, though I didn't really feel it.

George chimed in, looking relaxed and happy. "What's with the radio silence? How'd the pitch go this afternoon?"

"Great. Donelson signed the seven-book contract and is even treating me to dinner tonight." I tried to muster some enthusiasm, but it fell flat. "How's the skiing in Colorado?"

"Amazing!" Mary squealed. "It's so pretty here."

I could picture it—the snow-capped mountains, the crisp air, the kind of peace that only comes from being far away from everything. It felt like a million miles from where I was. "That's great, Mary. You have the whole week to enjoy it."

"It's been a blast, sis. We wish you were here," George said, his voice warm, but I could see a question in his eyes beneath it.

"I wish I was, too. There's just…a lot going on." I hesitated, the words sticking in my throat. "Edgar Shep died this morning."

George's response was gentle but matter-of-fact. "Sorry to

hear that. It was expected though, right? After that stroke, he just wasn't going to recover."

I nodded. "Yeah, it's probably a blessing. That's what everyone says, I guess. But still it doesn't really feel like it."

"Then why so glum, chum?"

I rolled my eyes, a small smile tugging at my lips despite myself. George always had a way of breaking through my defenses. I sighed, staring at the ceiling of my car as if it held the answers. "David and I...we sort of...hit things off this morning. A bit. I thought. But now..." The words hung heavy, unfinished. I still couldn't believe it. A thumbs up emoji as the only response to a career and business changing deal? It made no sense.

George knew me well enough to fill in the gaps. "You didn't. He's engaged. Jean, you're not—"

"No. He and Beth broke up. The engagement's off." My voice was firmer than I felt, trying to convince him, trying to convince myself.

"Is it really? Or is she just toying with him? We both know that's her way."

I bristled, the truth of his words striking a nerve. "David is done with her. He told me himself."

George's tone softened, but the skepticism remained. "Oh, I see. So you're wasting no time, huh? Snapping him up before someone else does?"

I closed my eyes. "We just—I don't know exactly. It's just beginning. He's grieving, and with Donelson, we're going to be swamped. Maybe it's not a good time." The realization stung. Was that why David hadn't responded like I'd expected? Was I moving too fast, pushing him when he needed space?

"Jean, you've been head over heels for him for years. Are you sure he can live up to what you've made him into?"

I swallowed hard, my throat tight. "I don't know. I just—I need to sleep. It's been a long day."

"Okay, but call us tomorrow. And take care of yourself."

"I will. Love you guys."

I hung up and slumped back against the seat, staring at the car roof. After a few moments, I pulled myself up by my bootstraps—or in my case, more like my strappy heels—and headed into the restaurant.

I checked my coat and told the maître d' in the foyer whom I was meeting, and he quickly spirited me away to the dining room. The small tables draped in cream linens, the low lighting from the vintage sconces, the soft hum of conversation and tinkling of a piano player in the bar created an intimate atmosphere that was almost disorienting given the company I was about to keep.

Frederick was already seated at a corner table, perfectly

framed by a large window that overlooked the twinkling lights of downtown. He looked every bit the powerful, self-made man I knew him to be—dark tailored suit, crisp light green shirt, no tie, and an open collar that made him look relaxed yet still ooze confidence from every inch of his six-foot-plus frame. He stood as soon as he saw me, a warm smile spreading across his face, and I was struck once again by how effortlessly charismatic he was.

"Jean," he greeted, his voice rich and welcoming. "You look stunning."

"Thank you," I replied, feeling the heat rise to my cheeks. I had picked my favorite black dress—simple, elegant, three-quarter sleeves with a low back that felt daring but not over the top. His appreciative gaze told me I'd made the right choice.

Frederick pulled out my chair with the kind of old-world courtesy that caught me off guard. I wasn't used to this kind of attention, and certainly not from someone like him. As I sat down, I took a deep breath, hoping to steady the thrum of excitement coursing through me. This was business, I reminded myself. Just business.

But when Frederick sat across from me, leaning in slightly as if our exchange was already a shared secret, I knew that wasn't entirely true.

"I'm glad you made it," he said, his eyes never leaving

mine. "After that presentation today, I couldn't wait to continue our conversation."

"Neither could I," I said honestly, smoothing a burgundy cloth napkin over my lap. Something about Frederick drew people in—his confidence was magnetic, and his interest in me felt genuine, like he wasn't just ticking off a social box but truly intrigued.

A waiter appeared, and Frederick ordered a bottle of vintage Bordeaux without consulting the menu. I raised an eyebrow. "You seem to know this place well." My nose suddenly began to run. I dabbed at it with the napkin.

"I met the chef," he said with a wink. "She's every bit as excellent as you described. I think you'll love what she has in store for us."

The wine arrived, deep red and fragrant, and Frederick watched me intently as I took my first sip. It was rich, velvety, with just a hint of something dark and spicy that lingered on my tongue. He smiled, as if my reaction pleased him.

I had to force myself to quit gazing back at him. I felt like some silly groupie from a rock band. I'd followed Frederick Donelson's career even before there'd been any remote chance he might need a publisher in his entourage. The adventures he'd documented online through blog and social media videos had me on the edge of my seat. No matter where he traveled, he always found a project to do some good, to benefit the local economy and population, no matter how advanced or primitive. Through my own research, I'd found that his humanitarian efforts spread far beyond what mainstream media publicized.

I blinked repeatedly, my eyes suddenly dry and itchy. I focused on the breathtaking view of Elmburn behind him, on the quiet couples dining around us, on the table décor, anywhere that would allow me to stop ogling him.

Glancing around, I noticed each table seemed to have a different flower in a bud vase: bright Gerber daisies, chrysanthemums, and asters. I brushed the edge of a single, heavy peach rose on our table with my fingertips. "Thank goodness we have this one."

"Why's that?" Frederick asked, taking a bite of a breadstick.

"I'm allergic to flowers in the daisy family. Looks like this is the only table without one." I wiped my nose again, embarrassed that it was starting to mimic a faucet.

He appeared alarmed. "How allergic?"

We were somewhat isolated at the corner table, but I always carried a stock of antihistamines in my purse. After catching the bridal bouquet at George's wedding years ago had nearly sent me into anaphylaxis, he'd urged me to get an epinephrine auto-injector prescription from a doctor. But I hadn't reacted as severely in years, so I'd just let it go.

"I should be fine if I don't get too close." As if on cue, I sneezed, hard. Three times in a row.

Frederick waved the waiter over. He pulled a few large bills from his wallet. "I don't want to see any flower in this restaurant that isn't a rose. Have one of your busboys or dishwashers go out and buy replacements—roses only. As soon as possible, please."

"Oh, that's not necessary," I began, but the itchiness in my eyes increased. I fought the urge to rub them and smear my mascara.

The waiter paid no attention to my protest. "Absolutely, Mr. Donelson. We'll do it immediately."

I felt a blush crawling up my neck. "Does everybody jump when you give an order?"

"Most do." His expression was humble, but then he grinned at me. "Then someone like you comes along."

"What does that mean?" I took an antihistamine out of the travel bottle in my purse, downing it quickly with my glass of water. Then I nibbled a breadstick as well.

"You make me doubt myself."

I almost choked on the dry, salty bite, and I grabbed for my water glass. After clearing my throat, I said breathlessly, "How could I possibly do that?"

He began to answer but was interrupted by the manager. "I apologize wholeheartedly for the flowers, Mr. Donelson. They are being removed as we speak." The manager of Amelie's restaurant looked like he'd stepped out of a vintage film reel, all slick hair and sharp angles, his bow tie cinched tight against the sweat glistening on his brow. He moved with the jittery energy of a man who's always one wrong step from a catastrophe—frazzled but trying to keep a thin veneer of charm intact. As he fumbled through his apology to Frederick about the poor choice in flowers, his eyes darted nervously, flitting between the table and Frederick's stony face.

Frederick nodded to the manager, his expression stoic but polite. "Thank you."

The manager scurried away, leaving us in an awkward silence. I twisted my napkin in my lap, searching Frederick's face for some sign that this wasn't completely over the top. But he looked perfectly composed, like ordering a floral overhaul of an entire restaurant was as natural as asking for a refill.

"I still don't see why you did that," I said, trying to mask my unease with a small smile.

Frederick leaned back in his chair, his brown eyes locked on mine. "I'd rather the restaurant be inconvenienced than see you get hurt or have to cut our time together short."

I blinked, unsure how to respond. It wasn't just what he'd

said—it was how he'd said it, like it was the most logical thing in the world.

"I'm only in town until tomorrow afternoon. Since I highly doubt you'd drop everything and jump on my plane with me back to Florida …" He paused, raising his eyebrows.

I gave him a short laugh as I wiped my nose again and shook my head.

He smiled and shrugged his shoulders. "See? We have to make the most of the time we have." His voice softened, almost tender. "And for the record, Jean, it's not about everyone jumping when I give an order. It's about being heard when it matters."

I took another sip of water and set my glass down, feeling the cool condensation on my fingertips.

Frederick chuckled, his grin sharp and knowing. "I think you'll keep me on my toes, Jean. I can't decide if it's intentional or just…you."

I raised an eyebrow, letting a teasing smile curl my lips. "Maybe you're just not used to someone pushing back."

"Oh, I've dealt with plenty of pushback," he said, his gaze lingering on me in a way that felt almost intimate. "But you— you're different. You don't just push; you make me think. And it's not something I'm used to liking."

"Is that a compliment or a warning?" I asked, my voice

softening.

"Both, maybe," he admitted, his tone quieter now, almost confessional. "You make me wonder if I've been settling for less. And with the life I've had, that's intriguing."

I hesitated, feeling the charged space between us. "I'm not trying to be difficult, you know."

Frederick's eyes held mine, warm and searching. "No, you're just being yourself, and that's exactly what's got me hooked."

His words hung between us, and I could feel my pulse quicken, an unfamiliar flutter taking root deep in my chest. Frederick's gaze was steady, unflinching, and for a moment, I let myself bask in the weight of it, in the warmth of being seen so clearly. There was something intoxicating about the way he looked at me—like I was a puzzle he was desperate to solve, a challenge he hadn't anticipated but couldn't resist.

And God help me, I liked it. I liked the way his attention wrapped around me, pulling me into his orbit. But then, like a cold slap of reality, the image of David flashed in my mind— David with his careful touch, his easy smile that masked a dozen secrets, the man who had finally kissed me breathless this morning and afternoon, which now felt a hundred years ago.

I suddenly disliked how I felt tethered to him—with a leash of my own making—how his absence was a lingering bruise that ached.

Frederick looked at me like I was something new and uncharted. I was drawn to his warmth, and a piece of me wanted to feel free to lean into whatever this was, but David's shadow was long, and I wasn't sure if I could ever outrun it— or if I even wanted to. I'd always preferred the cool of the shade to the heat of the sun.

Frederick took a sip of his wine. "So, tell me," he said, setting his glass down with deliberate care, "how does someone like you end up working at a place like Shep and Son?"

The question was pointed, but his tone was light, almost teasing. I took a moment, choosing my words carefully. "Well, it wasn't exactly a straight path," I said, swirling the wine in my glass. "I started with a bachelor's in English, thinking I had the next great American novel inside of me, but that wasn't to be. Then, I discovered that I've always been drawn to strategy, to creating narratives that make people see the best in something. I returned to Dartmouth and studied comparative literature.

"I was born and raised in Elmburn, and my brother asked if I'd consider staying close to home. His wife was dying from cancer, and, after college, I had stepped in to help them as much as I could.

"So I applied to a few places here, and Shep and Son gave me the chance to do what I wanted."

"How would you define what you wanted? Initially?"

I looked at the deep red of the wine in my glass and tried to find a way to explain it. "A creator's raw work is like the grapes that this wine started as. When it's grown just right, we harvest, crush and press, and ferment it. After some clarification and aging, we bottle the work between the covers of a book. And if we did our job right, when you consume it, it is going to satisfy you just as much as this does." I swirled the wine in the wide-mouth glass and took a sip. "Maybe even more so."

As he leaned in, resting his forearms on the table, I could feel the space between us narrow, like the room had somehow shrunk to contain just the two of us. His eyes stayed locked on mine, dark and inviting, pulling me in with every subtle shift in his expression. I watched the way his fingers traced the rim of his glass, slow and deliberate, mirroring the way his gaze traced over my face, studying me with an intensity that sent a warm flush creeping up my neck.

My breath hitched as his thumb brushed against his lower lip, and I couldn't help but wonder what that touch would feel like on my skin. I tucked a loose strand of hair behind my ear, a nervous gesture that felt far too telling, but I couldn't tear my eyes away.

I caught myself biting my lip, tasting the headiness of the wine, and I knew that whatever line we were dancing around was becoming thinner with every lingering glance, every stolen moment of silence that felt more like a promise than an accident.

"And what drives you? What's the fire underneath it all?" His voice was low and rich, each word laced with a hint of curiosity and something else—something that felt like desire, sparking with every exchange.

People rarely asked what truly motivated me—they usually just saw the polished exterior, the woman who knew her way around a boardroom. But Frederick's gaze was piercing like he was trying to see beyond my practiced smile.

"I want to make an impact," I said finally. "To take something ordinary and turn it into something unforgettable. I want to create things that last, that matter."

Frederick's smile broadened, and he raised his glass in a small toast. "That's exactly why I like you, Jean. You don't just talk about ideas; you breathe life into them."

His words sent a shiver down my spine. It was more than just a compliment—it felt like he truly saw me, saw the work I'd put in and the sacrifices I'd made. We clinked glasses, and for a moment, the rest of the restaurant faded away.

Dinner was a sensory experience that unfolded in stages, each course more elaborate and perfectly executed than the last. We started with an amuse-bouche of scallops drizzled in truffle oil. The main course was a succulent lamb, tender and spiced just right, paired with a medley of roasted vegetables that seemed to burst with flavor.

Frederick was an engaging conversationalist, effortlessly moving from one topic to the next. He told me stories about his travels—wild adventures in the Amazon jungles, sailing around the Mediterranean in a recreated Phoenician boat he had helped to build, and even a stint living with monks in Tibet. Every tale was tinged with humor and introspection, revealing a man who had seen the world in all its beauty and brutality.

As the evening wore on, I found myself drawn deeper into the orbit of Frederick's quiet charisma. He answered each of my questions with a thoughtfulness that caught me off guard—there was no rush, no glossing over the details. When I asked him why he'd spent time with monks, he didn't just give me a surface answer; he described the crisp mountain air, the echo of chanting through the monastery halls, and the profound silence that forced him to confront parts of himself he hadn't known were there.

"I wanted to understand stillness," he said, his voice soft yet firm, "to find out what was left when everything else was stripped away." It was the way he said it, with a quiet intensity that made me feel as if he were letting me in on some secret, some hidden layer of his soul.

Even when I asked about the more mundane—what it was like to navigate the bureaucracy of his family's business or his thoughts on the latest economic trends—he answered with a depth that made every subject feel significant, as though he was unearthing something meaningful in even the simplest of topics.

"The thing is, you can learn more about a person from the way they handle the little things than the big ones," he said, meeting my gaze. "The details matter—they're where the truth lies."

And in that moment, I realized it wasn't just his stories that captivated me; it was the way he seemed to live them fully, to pull every bit of experience from life, thoughtful and deliberate, making even the ordinary feel extraordinary. With every word, every lingering look, he was carving a space between us that felt impossibly intimate, and I tip-toed along the edge, like a girl playing on a balance beam, wondering if the fall would hurt.

"Life's too short to stay in one place," he said, cutting into his lamb. "I've always believed that if you're not moving forward, you're just wasting time."

I nodded, captivated not just by his stories but by the way he told them. He had a way of making me feel like I was right there with him, experiencing every high and low. It was no wonder he'd built an empire—people naturally gravitated toward him.

"And you?" he asked, refocusing on me. "Have you always played it safe, or have you had your share of adventures?"

I laughed, a little caught off guard by his directness. "I guess I've always been more calculated," I admitted. "But that doesn't mean I don't take risks. They're just...quieter ones."

Frederick leaned back, studying me with those sharp brown eyes. "Quieter risks can be the most dangerous, you know. Because they sneak up on you."

The air between us thickened, and I felt a sudden jolt of connection, as if he'd just touched on something deeper than either of us intended. The conversation shifted again, lighter now, but that moment lingered.

When dessert arrived—an indulgent dark chocolate soufflé that nearly defied gravity—Frederick's mood shifted slightly. He set his spoon down, his expression suddenly serious, and I braced myself for whatever was coming next.

"Jean," he began, his voice lower, more intimate. "Tonight's been incredible. I'm not just talking about the food or the wine. I mean you—your company, your presence. You're extraordinary."

I swallowed, my heart skipping a beat at the sincerity in his tone. I liked Frederick—more than I wanted to admit. He was charming, intelligent, and made me feel seen in a way that was rare. But I couldn't shake the feeling that this was moving too fast and that I was on the edge of something thrilling and terrifying.

"Thank you," I said, my voice softer now. "I've enjoyed tonight too."

He leaned closer, his gaze never wavering. "I don't just want to work with you, Jean. I want to know you, hopefully on an intimate level someday. And I won't pretend otherwise."

My breath hitched. The intensity of his words was undeniable. There was a spark between us—one I wouldn't have expected in a million years but couldn't deny.

Frederick reached out, brushing a loose strand of hair behind my ear. It was a small, almost tender gesture, but it sent a jolt of electricity through me. His touch was warm, lingering just long enough to make me feel flushed and slightly off balance.

"You deserve someone who sees you, Jean," he continued, his voice low and earnest. "Who appreciates everything you bring to the table, both in business and beyond."

I couldn't look away from him. It was like standing at the edge of a cliff, knowing you should back up but tempted to take the leap anyway. Frederick Donelson was dangerous—not in the obvious sense, but because he made me believe that every risk was worth taking.

"I…" I was unsure of what to say. He was right; I felt like

I'd spent so much of my life chasing things—first inclusion as a child, then education when it became clear that I'd never fit in the way I imagined I should, and then finally I'd chased the love of a man who had never truly seen me, who had chosen the woman who, for the better part of two decades, had been the bane of my existence. I thought my tireless works would have to win out in the end, and I'd forgotten what it felt like to be pursued for who I was rather than what I could do.

Frederick's expression softened, and he took my hand, his thumb brushing over my knuckles in a way that sent my pulse racing. "Jean, I don't do this lightly. But I want you to know—I'm interested. Definitely in working together and also in exploring whatever this is between us."

I stared at our joined hands, the reality of the moment sinking in. This was Frederick Donelson, a man who could have anything he wanted, and yet here he was, saying he wanted me. It was thrilling, but also terrifying. I had no idea what his interest could mean for me, for my career, for everything I'd built.

"I didn't expect this," I said, my voice barely above a whisper.

"Neither did I," he replied, smiling softly. "But sometimes the unexpected is exactly what we need."

He lifted my hand to his lips, pressing a gentle kiss to the back of it. The gesture was old-fashioned, romantic in a way that made my heart twist. It was a moment out of time, one that felt both wildly out of place and yet somehow perfectly right.

We left the restaurant together, the winter night causing a chill through my warmest coat and gloves. Frederick walked me to my vehicle, every step laced with the unspoken tension between us. As I fumbled with my keys, he caught my wrist, pulling me closer.

"I'll see you soon, Jean," he said, his voice a low promise.

And then, before I could second-guess anything, he leaned in and kissed me. It was brief, a brush of lips that left me breathless and wanting more. Frederick pulled back, his eyes searching mine, and I knew that this was just the beginning.

I watched him walk away, his figure disappearing into the night, and I stood there, heart pounding. This wasn't just dinner; it was the start of something I couldn't quite name but was certain would change everything.

***

*David*

The office building was dark and quiet, the kind of quiet that settles deep into your bones and makes you feel the weight of every thought. I'd driven here without thinking, too restless to sleep after a few hours of tossing and turning in bed. I parked in the empty lot, the city's neon glow flickering faintly through the windows, casting long, shadowed patterns on the walls. The Shep and Son building, normally bustling with life during the day, felt ghostly now—empty, hollow, like a shell of what it used to be. I unlocked the door and walked through the familiar halls, my footsteps echoing off the polished floors, the soft hum of the fluorescent lights the only company I had.

I found myself standing in the doorway of my office, looking at the desk that had been my battlefield for years. Papers were still strewn across it, remnants of the Donelson pitch Jean and I had worked on so tirelessly. The whiteboard was filled with numbers and scrawled notes, half-erased reminders of the hours we'd spent here, side by side, fighting to keep this place afloat. I ran a hand through my hair, tugging at the strands in frustration. I couldn't get her out of my mind. *Jean.* The one person who had been my constant through it all.

I slumped into my chair, swiveling slightly as I stared at the ceiling, trying to piece together the chaos of my thoughts. Jean had been everything today—smart, focused, a calming presence when everything felt like it was falling apart. I couldn't stop thinking about the way she'd kissed me this afternoon, her lips soft but urgent, like she was trying to anchor us both. I closed my eyes, letting the memory wash over me—the taste of her, the warmth of her touch. It had been so long since I'd felt anything that real. Six years we'd worked together, and I'd been too cautious to take hold of what was right in front of me.

I remembered the first time I'd met Jean—fresh out of Dartmouth, eager and full of ideas. She'd come into the office with that determined glint in her eye, not intimidated by the legacy of Shep and Son or by the towering presence of my father. She was different, in all the ways that mattered. Where I saw problems, she saw possibilities. Where I lost my temper, she found solutions. And through it all, she'd never once wavered. Not when my father had undermined every decision I made, not when the company's future looked grim, and certainly not when my own life started to unravel.

I thought about all the times Jean had been there, quietly picking up the pieces I'd left behind. The late nights working on deadlines, the quiet cups of coffee she'd placed on my desk without a word, the countless times she'd calmed my frayed nerves with just a look. She'd always been there, steady and unflinching, even when I didn't deserve it—especially when I didn't deserve it. I ran my hand over my face, feeling the roughness of stubble and the exhaustion that clung to me like a second skin.

I glanced around the room, my eyes landing on a photo of my father on the shelf, looking out with that same stern expression he always wore. Edgar Shep, the man who had worked side by side with his own father to build this company from the ground up, who had been both my idol and my greatest source of pain. I snatch the picture off the shelf and sat back down, tracing the frame's edges with my thumb, my throat tightening. It had been two months since his stroke, and now he was gone. Just like that. And all I felt was this gnawing emptiness, this bitter regret that I couldn't shake.

I'd spent my whole life trying to live up to his expectations, trying to be the son he could be proud of, and now I was left with nothing but the echoes of all the things I'd never said. I hated him for the way he'd belittled me too often, always made me feel like nothing I did was good enough. But more than that, I hated myself for still caring, for still wanting his approval even now, when it was far too late.

I set the photo down, feeling the weight of it settle back into my chest. I wanted to call Jean, to hear her voice, to tell her everything I was feeling—the grief, the anger, the mess I'd made of my life. But she'd asked for space, for time to figure out what this thing between us was, and I owed her that much at least.

But I wanted to drive over to her house, to knock on her door and just let it all out, but I knew I couldn't. Not now. Not when I was barely holding it together. What a goddamn wreck I was.

I turned my chair, staring out the window at the empty

streets below. The city never really slept, but tonight it felt like it was holding its breath, waiting for something I couldn't name. I picked up my phone, scrolling through old messages from Jean, all the little check-ins and reminders she'd sent over the past couple of months. I could feel her presence even in those small, thoughtful gestures. She was always thinking of me, always one step ahead, and I couldn't help but wonder how I'd been so blind.

I thought about the night my father first got sick, how Jean had been the one to find him collapsed on the office floor. She'd called me after the ambulance, her voice shaking, but she'd handled everything with a calmness I couldn't muster. I hadn't even thanked her properly. I'd been too caught up in my own anger, too wrapped up in my own pain to see how much she was hurting too. Jean had always been the one holding things together, and I'd taken that for granted. I'd taken her for granted.

The clock on my computer screen flickered, reminding me how late it was, but sleep was the last thing on my mind. I paced the office, feeling the pull of memories in every corner. I thought about all the times I'd let Jean down, all the moments I'd been too wrapped up in my own bullshit to appreciate everything she did. And now, when I needed her most, she was the one person I couldn't reach out to.

I walked over to her office, the door slightly ajar, as if she'd just stepped out. Her desk was neat, organized, a stark contrast to the chaos of mine. I ran my fingers along the edge, feeling the smooth surface, imagining her sitting there, focused and intent. A stack of manuscripts lay on the corner, notes in her neat handwriting scribbled in the margins. She'd always had this way of making sense of the mess, of finding the thread that pulled everything together.

I sat in her chair, letting the familiar scent of her perfume—that warm ginger and amber—wash over me. It felt wrong to be here without her, like I was intruding on something private. But I couldn't bring myself to leave. I leaned back, closing my eyes, and let the memories flood in. Jean laughing at one of my stupid jokes, Jean bringing me a sandwich when I'd forgotten to eat, Jean sitting across from me at the conference table, her green eyes bright with ideas and determination.

She was one of a kind. There was no one else like her. Her kindness, her generosity, the way she put up with all my flaws and never once made me feel like I was too much. She'd stood by me through every failure, every misstep, and I didn't know how to tell her how much that meant. I didn't know how to tell her that she was the best part of my life, the one thing that made all of this bearable.

My gut churned. I was afraid. Afraid of pushing her away,

afraid that I'd already asked too much of her. She deserved more than this—more than me.

The low lights in the hallway weren't strong enough to illuminate the words on the framed Dickinson poem she'd hung on the wall a few years ago. But they didn't need to. I'd read it more times than I could count, and the haunting words had become synonymous with Jean herself. Just four simple stanzas that spoke of the profoundness of not realizing what you had before it was taken away from you.

I stood up, looking around her office one last time before heading back to mine. The silence was suffocating now, the walls closing in with every second that passed. I sank back into my chair, staring at the darkened screen of my phone. I knew I needed to give her space, but every instinct in me screamed to reach out, to not let this slip away.

I pulled up my recent contacts again, my thumb hovering over the call button, but I couldn't do it. Not yet. Not when I was still tangled up in all this grief, all this regret. I tossed the phone onto the desk and buried my face in my hands, feeling the weight of everything pressing down on me. I wished I could share this with her, let her in, but I was terrified of what she might see.

The hours dragged on, the office growing colder, the shadows stretching longer. I closed my eyes, trying to find some peace in the quiet, but all I could think about was Jean—her smile, her touch, the way she made me feel like maybe, just maybe, I was worth saving. And all I could do was hope that when she was ready, when we were both ready, she'd still be there. Because without her, this place, this life—it didn't mean a damn thing.

***

*Beth*

I leaned back against the royal blue velvet booth, sinking into the plushness. The bar was alive with people who looked like they'd stepped straight out of a magazine—designer suits, sequined dresses, and all the glitter that money could buy. It was the kind of place where being seen was the whole point, where every flash of a camera or snap of a selfie was a declaration of relevance. The music throbbed, loud and bass-heavy, vibrating through the floor and up into my bones, but it was the power that buzzed through my veins that really set me alight. My friends were all around me, tossing back shots, laughing too loudly, and soaking up the attention of the crowd. But my mind was somewhere else, savoring the quiet thrill of my little game.

David had been a brick wall through dinner. Every tactic, every method that had always worked to break into him

99

previously had failed. In the end, unfortunately, it had been just a meal. He acted like he couldn't wait to get me out the door, and my brain was busy scheming hard to figure out how to deal with this new armored side of him.

I glanced down at my phone, my lips curling into a smirk as I watched Jean's late-night sleepless message come through, thanks to the contact card changes I had made on both of their phones.

*Hoping no news is good news. Call me in the morning.*

I didn't bother sending it on to David. I could practically hear the whiny tension in her voice. It was perfect. She thought she was texting David, spilling out her confusion and insecurity, everything between the lines that made her so wonderfully weak right now.

And David, bless his naive heart, was doing exactly what I'd hoped he would—stepping further and further away, attempting to handle it all on his own, doubting, doubting, doubting. Every message they sent was a tangled noose of miscommunication that I was tightening, little by little, until it would finally hang them both.

I tucked my phone back into my clutch, the screen glowing faintly against the sequins of my dress. God, this was too easy. David and Jean, two little puppets dancing on strings that I controlled, completely oblivious. All it took was a little change to their contact cards, a quick swap that had been laughably simple to pull off while David was in the shower this afternoon. They were too caught up in each other to even suspect it.

I sipped my drink, the rum burning sweetly down my throat. They were right where I needed them—confused, disconnected, and teetering on the edge of something deliciously destructive. A little more time, a few more carefully crafted replies, and I'd be able to drop the hammer, breaking them apart once and for all. Jean thought she could just waltz in and take everything that was mine, like she always had. But she didn't know the rules of this game. She didn't understand that the only way to get what you want is to be willing to do whatever it takes.

I learned that from my mom. I watched her play this game long before I ever did. She was a master at it—manipulation, deceit, little moves that shifted everything in her favor. I could still remember the way she'd cornered Jean's dad, pressing him with sweet words and half-smiles, playing him like the fool he was.

Jean and George's dad was a mess when my mom found him, vulnerable and weak, but she'd seen potential. She knew exactly how to push, how to pull, until he was so tangled up in her schemes that he couldn't see straight. She'd made him believe that every decision was his own, every misstep a twist of fate rather than the careful guiding of her hand.

I used to sit at the top of the stairs, listening as she talked to him in the kitchen, her voice syrupy and smooth, always laced with just enough sadness or sweetness to get what she wanted. One night, she caught me watching, my small frame hidden behind the banister, and instead of scolding me, she'd winked.

"It's all about the long game, sweetheart," she said later on, her smile sharper than any knife. "You've got to make them think they're in control. That's when you really have them."

Those words stuck. I saw her work her way into that man's life, piece by piece, until she'd taken everything she wanted. The house, the money, the status—my mom played the game better than anyone. And when it all fell apart, when Jean's dad finally saw through the smoke and mirrors, it was too late. He was ruined, and Mom walked away without a backward glance. I never forgot the way she'd looked that day, her chin high, her eyes fierce, unbothered by the wreckage she'd left behind. It was survival. It was power.

Now, sitting in this crowded bar, watching my friends flirt and dance under the neon lights, I felt that same rush. Jean had always been the golden child, the one everyone praised while I was left to claw my way up from nothing. She thought she'd won, taking David, worming her way into his life like she deserved it. But she was just like her father—easily led, easily fooled. I was going to tear her down the way my mom had done with her dad, and this time, there'd be no coming back.

"Beth, you're so quiet tonight!" Amanda, one of my oldest friends, leaned over, her breath hot with vodka and lime. "What's going on in that pretty little head of yours?"

I flashed her a grin, letting the corners of my mouth pull up just enough to be playful. "Oh, nothing," I said, lifting my glass. "Just thinking about some unfinished business."

Amanda rolled her eyes, laughing as she tossed her blonde hair over her shoulder. "You and your drama," she teased. "What happened to just living in the moment?"

I clinked my glass against hers, the ice rattling. "I am living in the moment," I said, watching her sip her drink, her eyes already glazed with tipsiness. "But a girl's gotta keep her eyes on the prize."

Amanda didn't get it. None of them did. To them, this was just another night out, another string of flings and fleeting moments. But to me, every second was a move, every glance a calculation. I wasn't here to just have fun—I was here to win.

I pulled out my phone again, scrolling through the messages from David and Jean, the ones they thought they were sending to each other. Another message from Jean blinked back at me, full of her stupid, doe-eyed sincerity.

*I just want you to know I'm here for you, no matter what.*

It made me sick. She thought she could be his savior, his rock, when really she was just another problem he couldn't solve. She'd receive no response to anything she sent tonight. Let her doubt. Let her suffer.

David, meanwhile, was practically unraveling. He'd never admit it, but ever since his father's stroke, he was terrified of losing control, terrified of letting someone else see how broken he really was. And I was there, the ever-present reminder of his flaws, feeding him just enough validation to keep him on the hook. He'd never be strong enough for Jean, and he knew it. I'd make sure he knew it.

My phone buzzed with a new notification, a comment on my latest post. I'd made sure to take a picture on David's bed when he was showering this afternoon, letting the soft filter and strategically placed sheets imply exactly what I wanted. It didn't matter that nothing had happened—what mattered was the story I was crafting, the image I was putting out there. The comments were predictable: friends cheering me on, hinting at things they thought they understood. Jean had seen it too, I knew she had, and it would eat away at her like poison. She wouldn't confront David directly, not yet, but the doubt would fester, and soon, it would be too much.

I glanced up, watching my friends dance to a song I barely recognized. They were lost in the music, in the thrill of the night, but I was somewhere else entirely. My mother's voice echoed in my mind, reminding me of the lessons she'd taught me without ever saying a word. People were easy to manipulate, easy to control, as long as you knew where to press. And right now, I was pressing all the right buttons.

"Beth!" Amanda called out, waving me over to the bar. "Come on, shots!"

I pushed my phone back into my clutch, sliding out of the booth and strutting across the crowded floor. I could feel eyes on me—men watching, women whispering—and I soaked it up, every ounce of attention a reminder that I was in control. I was the one calling the shots, and no one was going to take that away from me.

Not Jean. Not David. Not anyone.

I raised my glass with the girls, throwing back the shot and feeling the burn of tequila, the rush of power that surged through me. This was my game, and I was winning.

I leaned against the bar, reveling in the music pulsing around me, and I couldn't help but laugh. It was all so easy.

***

*Jean*


*I reached for the bell trying to silence it. I didn't want to leave, not yet. It was my turn. Everyone was there—Beth, Edgar, George, Mary, my co-workers—sitting in oddly small school desks. The old-fashioned kind in pictures of one-room schoolhouses with wooden tops that sported coarse grain and connected chairs. We were all waiting for David to walk through the door. I had been sent to the back of the room, made to sit in the last row. I made a swipe for the bell again, but I was stuck to my chair.*

*Everyone else stood up, laughing and pointing at me. They each grabbed a pop bottle on the way out of the room and threw it at me. Then they left me. I was alone, the bell dinging in my ears, waiting for David to show up.*

I woke from the ridiculous nightmare in a cold sweat. Rolling over, I buried my face in the pillow, but there was no escaping the memories that came rushing back unbidden. Beth's taunting and attacks, sometimes physical. Always emotional. I had to tell myself, just as I had through all those years, that as much as she hurt me, she was hurting even more from something.

I took a deep breath, picked up my phone, and started scrolling through news headlines as was my normal routine. At the bottom of the home page, I saw Edgar Shep's name listed under *Obituaries*. His death still didn't feel real. The service had been scheduled four days from now but there was no obituary yet to accompany it. My eyes filled with tears.

I hadn't expected it to hit me this hard, the reality of him being gone. Edgar was more than just my boss; he was my mentor, the kind of person who made you feel like you were exactly where you were supposed to be.

I could still remember my first day at Shep and Son, almost like it had happened yesterday. I was so nervous I could barely breathe, my stomach twisted into knots as I stood in the elevator, watching the numbers tick up to the top, to the fifth floor. I clutched my bag tightly, feeling the weight of every doubt and insecurity I'd carried with me since graduating. What if I wasn't good enough? What if they figured out I was a fraud?

When the doors opened, I stepped into the buzzing chaos of the busiest floor of the publishing house. Phones rang, papers shuffled, and conversations hummed in the background. I had no idea where to go or what to do. The receptionist waved me over with a smile and pointed me in the direction of Edgar's office. He was waiting for me, standing in the doorway with his hand extended and a warm, welcoming smile that immediately put me at ease.

"Jean, right? Edgar Shep. I'm so glad you're here."

His voice was kind, with that gruff undertone of a man who had spent decades in the business. There was an immediate sense of authority about him, but also a gentleness that made you feel like you were being let into something special. I shook his hand, grateful for the steady grip that seemed to ground me.

We spent the next hour going over my role, the projects I'd be working on, and what he expected from me. He spoke with such passion about the industry, about stories and writers and the magic of bringing books into the world. Edgar had a way of making everyone around him believe in the power of words, that what we were doing mattered in a way that was bigger than just turning a profit.

He told me stories of the early days, of how he and his father had built the company from the ground up, and his voice would light up with a pride that was contagious. By the end of that first meeting, I was inspired, not just by the job, but by him.

Then came the second hour of my first day, and everything changed. I was sitting at my new desk, trying to familiarize myself with the manuscript stacks, and I felt slightly less panicked when the office door opened. David Shep walked in.

I looked up from my work, and it felt like the whole world went quiet. David had a presence about him, too. Similar to his father's but with a few major differences. His magnetism drew every eye in the room, including mine. He was tall, blonde, with striking blue eyes that seemed to pierce right through you. There was something effortless about him.

He glanced around the office, eyes scanning the room with a kind of disinterest until they landed on me. I remember the moment so vividly, the way our eyes met, and my breath caught in my throat. It was like something out of a movie, that ridiculous cliché of love at first sight that I'd never believed in until that second. I'd like to say I played it cool, but I was a deer caught in the headlights, my cheeks flushing as I realized I was staring.

"Hi," he said, his voice smooth and casual. "You must be the new junior editor. Jean, right?"

I nodded, my mouth suddenly too dry to form words. He was even more handsome up close, with a sharp jawline and a smile that hinted at mischief. I was struck by the easy charm he carried, the way he made you feel like you were the only person in the room.

He introduced himself, though of course, I already knew who he was—David Shep, Edgar's son, the heir apparent to the family business. But he wasn't what I expected. He wasn't just the boss's son waltzing through the office with entitlement. There was a warmth to him, a charisma that was both genuine and disarming.

He asked about my first day, made a joke about the coffee being strong enough to strip paint, and laughed when I admitted I'd already had two cups. We talked for a few minutes, but it felt like longer, each second stretching out as I tried to soak in every detail. I was smitten, plain and simple. I'd spent years focusing on my education and the career I wanted to build, but here was David, and suddenly, all my priorities seemed to shift. It wasn't just his looks—though those didn't hurt—but the way he listened, the way he seemed genuinely interested in what I had to say. I'd never felt such an instant connection with anyone.

When he left, I watched him go, my heart hammering in my chest. It was the beginning of something, though I couldn't have known then just how complicated it would become. Over the next few years, Edgar became more than just my boss—he became a mentor, a confidant, someone who believed in me even when I doubted myself. And David? David became everything I didn't know I was looking for. He was brilliant and frustrating and wonderful all at once. I fell hard and fast, and despite everything that had happened since, I'd never stopped feeling that pull.

Now, my heart ached with the loss of Edgar and the uncertainty with David. I squeezed my eyes shut, wishing I could go back to that first day, when everything felt new and full of possibility. But there was no going back. There was only today, and the messy, tangled future that lay ahead.

My phone buzzed. It was a text from David!

*Hey Jean. You did so amazing on the Donelson project, why don't you just take a few days off? You've earned it. I don't want to see you in the office until next week.*

I sat straight up in bed. What the hell?! None of this made any sense. Tears filled my eyes and my head spun. I threw myself back down on my pillows. What was I supposed to do?

*** 

*David*

I sat at my desk, staring blankly at the blinking cursor on my laptop screen. The empty document mocked me, the header reading only "Obituary: Edgar Shep." I'd typed those words over an hour ago and hadn't managed a single sentence since. The office around me buzzed with its usual rhythm of voices, phones, and the occasional hum of the copy machine, but it all sounded distant, like a muffled background track to the turmoil inside my head.

I was supposed to be writing my father's obituary. I thought I could handle it, thought I could somehow sum up the life of Edgar Shep, the man who had built this company from scratch, who had mentored so many, who had guided me—however imperfectly—through a tumultuous father-son relationship. But as I sat there, fingers poised over the keyboard, nothing came. The words were stuck somewhere deep, trapped behind a wall of grief and guilt that I didn't know how to break through.

I rubbed my temples, the dull ache from too many sleepless nights radiating through my skull. I glanced at my phone on the desk, half hoping to see a message from Jean, but there was nothing. She'd been distant since the morning we'd almost...well, whatever we'd almost been.

She hadn't shown up to the meeting at the funeral home this morning, and I'd spent the first half-hour pacing the sidewalk, phone in hand, waiting for her. Every vehicle that neared, I glanced up, expecting her to breeze in with that calm, reassuring smile she always had, but Jean never came.

Instead, Beth had shown up, walking over from the dress shop across the street where she'd been trying on clothes for some charity gala. She'd seen me pacing and, for once, hadn't launched into her usual caustic commentary about my obvious distress. Instead, she'd simply walked up and said, "Do you need someone?"

I'd been too surprised to answer at first, and before I knew it, we were sitting in the funeral home together. Beth had been surprisingly helpful, handling some of the paperwork and keeping the conversation on track when my mind kept drifting.

But she wasn't Jean. She was never Jean. It was Jean I needed, Jean who knew my father almost as well as I did, Jean who would have understood the weight of every decision without needing it spelled out.

Now, Jean hadn't come in to work today. Technically, she was on scheduled vacation days, and with our marathon weekend, she deserved it. She was probably sleeping. I wanted to be.

I sighed, my hands falling to the desk. My phone buzzed, but it was just another reminder about an upcoming meeting. I shoved it aside and turned back to the laptop, staring at the blank page. My eyes stung with frustration, a burn that had less to do with the screen and more to do with the overwhelming sense of failure clawing at me. How could I not even do *this*? How could I not put together a few paragraphs about the man who had shaped my entire world?

But every time I tried, my mind flooded with memories that were too raw, too personal—Dad at his desk, poring over manuscripts with a magnifying glass when his eyesight began to fail; Dad teaching me to swing a bat as a kid, more patient than I'd ever seen him; Dad at the hospital, frail and distant, but still gripping my hand with what little strength he had left. It was too much.

Without thinking, I clicked on my email, not sure what I was looking for until I found myself opening a new message. I hesitated, then typed Jean's name in the recipient box. My fingers hovered over the keys, uncertain. This was too long for a text. I needed her to know everything, but I didn't even know where to start.

I took a deep breath and began typing.

*Subject: I Need Your Help*

*Jean,*

*I've started this email a dozen times, trying to find the right words. I'm not sure there are any. First, I want to say that I'm sorry. I'm sorry if you got the wrong impression the other afternoon with Beth. I know how that must have looked, but I promise, there's nothing between us. There hasn't been for a long time, and there never will be again. I don't want her back. I thought I made that clear to myself, but maybe I haven't done a good job of making it clear to you.*

*The truth is, she just showed up. I was waiting for you at the funeral home, pacing up and down that damn sidewalk. I kept thinking any second you'd appear and save me like you always do. But you didn't, and when Beth came over, I didn't have the energy to send her away. She sat with me, and I appreciate that she helped, but she's not you. She never will be.*

*I've been struggling, Jean. I thought I could write my dad's obituary. I thought I could find the words to capture who he was, but every time I try, I feel like I'm failing him all over again. He deserves more than what I can put together right now.*

*I know you loved him too, and I know you always saw the best in him, even when I couldn't. You've always had this clear, loving view of him, and I think that's what people need to hear. Not just from a son who's too tangled up in his own feelings, but from someone who really understood him.*

*I can't do this alone. I know I've asked a lot from you already, and I know this is no small thing. But you've always been the voice I needed when I couldn't find my own.*

*I'm so grateful to you, Jean, more than I can say. You saved us with that Donelson pitch. I was a wreck, and you pulled it off like it was nothing. I know that deal has saved our company's future. It's not just that, though. You saved my father's business legacy, and I'll always owe you for that.*

*I typed here that I owe you my heart, but maybe that's too much to say right now. I think I've screwed things up so badly that even saying it feels like I'm asking too much. But you should know—there isn't a day that goes by when I'm not thankful for you. You're the best thing that's ever happened to me, and I don't want you to feel like you're an afterthought.*

*So, I guess what I'm really asking is… would you consider writing the obituary? Would you help me do this one last thing for my dad? Because right now, I'm stuck. I'm stuck, and I don't know how to move forward without you.*

*I hope you'll say yes, but if you don't, I understand. Either way, thank you, Jean. For everything.*

*David*

I reread the email half a dozen times, my chest tightening as I hovered over the send button. I'd poured everything into those words, even the parts I couldn't quite bring myself to say out loud. I glanced at the line where I'd told her I owed her my heart and thought about deleting it. Was it cowardice? Was it just the wrong time? I didn't know. I only knew that Jean deserved better than mixed signals and half-truths.

I clicked send, the whoosh of the email leaving my outbox feeling like a finality I wasn't ready for. I sat back in my chair, staring at the screen, willing a response to appear. All I could do now was wait and hope that Jean would understand. That she would still be the Jean I needed, the Jean who could see through all the mess and help me find my way.

I leaned back, the office noise flooding back into my awareness. The obituary still loomed on my screen, blank and accusing. I closed the document, unable to face it any longer. Instead, I looked out the window, watching the city pulse with life beyond the glass. My office felt too small, too stifling, and all I wanted was to see Jean's name light up my screen with a promise that, somehow, things would be okay.

For now, I could only pray that she would find the words I couldn't, and maybe, just maybe, find it in her heart to forgive me for being an idiot for the last six years.

# Chapter Four

*Jean*

I parked my vehicle on Main Street, the engine ticking in the cold as I stared at the row of shops I'd passed a hundred times before but never stepped inside. Elmburn was chock full of places I always said I'd check out "someday," but work and life kept me too busy for such leisurely indulgences. Now, with an unexpected stretch of time off and the need to keep my mind from spiraling, today was that "someday."

I stepped out into the crisp air, the sky a soft winter gray, and pulled my coat tighter. The first shop I wandered into was a little bookstore with a bell that tinkled softly as the door opened. It was the kind of place that smelled like paper and dust, with shelves that leaned slightly under the weight of secondhand novels and coffee table books. I browsed aimlessly, running my fingers along the spines of old hardcovers, picking up one or two that caught my eye, but mostly just soaking in the quiet.

From there, I moved on to a tiny artisan bakery with pastries displayed like little works of art. I ordered a lavender scone that was almost too pretty to eat and sat by the window, watching people bustle by, lost in their own little worlds. The scone was a creative delicacy, and I savored it, realizing how nice it was to just sit and be. To feel normal. To pretend I was just another person with nothing more pressing than how much sugar was in my tea.

By lunch, I found myself at a new bistro on the corner, tucked between a florist and a vintage clothing shop. The kind of place with reclaimed wood tables and Edison bulbs hanging from the ceiling. I ordered a beet salad that tasted like earth and vinegar and sipped at an herbal tea that promised calm. The food was as satisfying through flavor as it was through new experience, and for the first time in days, I wasn't drowning in thoughts of David, Edgar, or anything beyond the next bite.

The ice rink kept nagging at the back of my mind as it had all morning. It had been years since I'd skated—since George and I were teenagers, weaving in and out of the local rink on those cold, winter evenings when we'd had nothing better to do. The pull was undeniable today. It was busy when I arrived, kids clumsily learning how to balance, couples gliding hand in hand, and a few older folks, stoic and steady, making their rounds.

I laced up my rental skates, the white leather stiff and unfamiliar, and wobbled onto the ice, feeling the cold glide beneath me. At first, I was awkward, my feet unsure as they found their rhythm, but after a few laps, it started to come back. I felt the breeze on my face, the smooth rhythm of my blades carving into the ice, and it was almost meditative, each stroke a beat that drowned out the noise in my head.

After a while, my ankles ached and the tips of my fingers were numb, so I shuffled off the ice and found a bench near the rink, cradling a cup of hot cocoa between my hands. The steam curled up in delicate tendrils, and I let the warmth seep through my gloves as I watched the skaters loop around in messy circles. I took a slow sip, savoring the too-sweet chocolate and the sticky, melty marshmallow.

I reached for my phone, out of habit more than anything. No missed calls. No texts. David's silence was deafening, a constant, nagging reminder that something was broken between us. I tapped my email app, scrolling absently until his name jumped out at me, the subject line plain and direct: *I Need Your Help.*

I opened the email, and my heart sank as I read his words. He'd needed me at the funeral home. He'd waited, paced the sidewalk expecting me to show up—but he hadn't asked me to be there. I couldn't believe it. The extent of our miscommunication hit me like a punch to the gut. I would have run through fire to be there with him, but he hadn't asked, and I hadn't known.

I read through his apology, his plea for help with the obituary, and my chest tightened. David was struggling, and I'd let my own insecurities keep me away. Maybe the stress and lack of sleep were affecting him more than I'd realized. He wasn't himself, and neither was I.

I stared down at my cocoa, swirling the marshmallows around with the tip of my finger, trying to process it all. I'd started a draft of Edgar's obituary weeks ago, back when the doctor had first told us to prepare. I'd kept it saved on my phone, half-finished, too painful to complete until now.

I opened it, scrolling through my notes and memories, and let myself remember Edgar in a way only I could. The way he'd guided me when I first started at Shep and Son, the way he'd believed in my instincts even when I doubted myself. How he'd tell stories about the early days of publishing that would make me laugh and feel like I was part of something much bigger.

I revised and refined, each word a small tribute to the man who had been so much more than my boss. I felt the tears come as I wrote, but it was cathartic, a way to say goodbye. When I was done, I hit send and watched it leave my outbox, my chest a mix of relief and heartache.

Moments later, my email app boasted a new message—a reply from David. His response was short, but it said everything I needed to hear: *Where are you?*

My fingers hovered over the screen, unsure of what to say. I hesitated, then typed back, *The skating rink.* I could practically feel his urgency in the seconds that followed, and then his reply came through: *I'm leaving right now.*

I stared at the screen, my heart hammering. Part of me wanted to bolt, to run from whatever this moment would turn into, but another part of me knew that running wouldn't solve anything. We needed to talk, face to face. We needed to bridge the gap that had grown between us, to confront whatever was left unsaid.

I put my phone away and took another sip of cocoa, the warmth soothing against my throat. I watched the skaters glide by, their laughter and shouts echoing off the rink walls. I tried to relax, to focus on the simple joy of being there, of doing something that made me feel like a kid again. But the tension was there, a knot that wouldn't quite loosen, because I knew that any minute, David would walk through those doors, and nothing would be the same.

I wrapped my hands tighter around the cup, feeling the heat seep through to my palms, and braced myself. I'd wait for him. For us. Because despite everything—despite the missed signals, the silence, and the confusion—I still believed in whatever this was between us. David needed me, and I needed him, and maybe it was time we both stopped running from that truth.

I looked up, watching the entrance, and took a deep breath. The cocoa was almost gone, but I held on to the cup, letting its warmth be the thing that kept me grounded, kept me there, waiting.

***

David

I could hardly see through the tears welling in my eyes as I pulled into the parking lot of the skating rink. On the way over, I'd listened to Jean's obituary for my father, playing it through my car's Bluetooth with the text-to-speech app. Her words had filled the car like music, capturing Edgar Shep in a way I could never have hoped to. Every sentence was perfect; every memory she wrote about him felt alive—vibrant and full of the grace that my own grief had clouded me from seeing. I'd gripped the steering wheel so hard my fingers were numb, trying to keep the tears at bay, but it was no use. She'd brought him back to me, if only for a moment.

She strategically wove his early years together, including details I'd forgotten about and some he had never bothered to share with me—or I'd just never bothered to ask. She hit the nail on the head when she explained the importance of Shep and Son to Edgar, how he'd always placed weight in being a part of something bigger than himself, something special. Jean had painted him as the mentor, the father, the man he truly was— not the shell I'd seen in his final days, not the distant figure I'd struggled to understand my whole life. She'd made him real again, and I felt like I was losing him all over.

I had barely managed to stop crying when I pulled into the parking lot, swiping at my eyes and taking a few deep breaths to steady myself. My heart still ached, a heavy, painful throb that pulsed through my chest as I stepped out of the car. I couldn't wait another second to see her. She'd brought my father back to life with her words, and now I needed to find her, to tell her what she'd done for me, for him. For us.

I pushed through the rink doors, the sharp scent of ice and the sounds of laughter and skates scraping against the frozen surface washing over me. The place was crowded, filled with families, couples, and kids stumbling along the ice, but Jean wasn't among them. I scanned the rink, my eyes darting from face to face, my pulse quickening with each second she was out of sight. She wasn't skating, wasn't near the clusters of teenagers taking selfies near the boards. Panic nipped at me, the fear of losing her again after the last few days of silence and miscommunication.

I moved around the rink, weaving through the crowd, my breath hitching each time I thought I spotted her. I'd come all this way, my heart in pieces, desperate to see her, and she was nowhere. My steps quickened, frantic, until finally, I spotted her—sitting off to the side, alone at a small table near the rink's edge. She wore her salt and pepper wool coat, the one that always made her look so put-together, so perfectly Jean. Her head was bowed slightly as she cradled a styrofoam cup, staring out at the skaters with a distant look in her eyes.

I couldn't stop the flood of emotions as I approached her, my footsteps slowing as I took her in. The sight of her there, so calm, so Jean, sent a wave of relief crashing over me. My heart pounded, every beat reminding me just how much I needed her, how much I'd always needed her. She looked up as I neared, her eyes meeting mine, and everything else in the world faded away.

I didn't say a word. I didn't know how to start, didn't know what words would do justice to everything I was feeling. Instead, I just reached for her, pulling her up from her seat and into my arms. She was warm, soft, and familiar, and the moment she was against me, I knew this was where I was supposed to be. Without thinking, I cupped her face in my hands, my fingers grazing her cheeks, and I kissed her—hard and desperate, all the pent-up longing and confusion pouring into that one searing kiss.

For a second, she melted into me, her lips moving against mine like she'd been waiting for this, too. But then she pulled back, her eyes searching mine, and I could feel the distance between us, a gap I hadn't been able to close no matter how much I wanted to.

She said my name softly, her voice carrying a touch of something I couldn't quite place—hesitation, maybe, or uncertainty.

I tightened my grip on her, unwilling to let her go, and rested my forehead against hers. "Jean, I'm sorry. I'm sorry for everything. For not being there the way you needed me to be. For… for whatever I did to make you think you were anything less than the most important person in my life."

She looked away, biting her lip, and I felt my chest tighten. "It's not about that. It's just… there's been so much, and I don't know how to sort through it all."

I reached out, brushing a stray strand of hair behind her ear. "Tell me what you need. If you want to skate, I'll skate with you. If you want to make love, I'll take you home right now. If you want to fly away, I'll take you to the airport and it'll just be the two of us. We can leave everything behind." My voice cracked, my words desperate and raw. "Just… let me fix this. Let me be whatever you need."

She stared at me, her eyes softening, and for a moment, I thought she might pull away again. But instead, she smiled—small, hesitant, but real. "Let's start with skating," she said quietly.

I nodded, swallowing the lump in my throat as I took her hand. We moved to the rental counter, trading my Oxfords for skates, and laced up on a bench. I watched her out of the corner of my eye, the way she tucked a loose strand of hair behind her ear in that habitual gesture I'd seen a thousand times. I couldn't stop looking at her, drinking in every little detail, every small piece of the woman I'd loved for so long and never quite figured out how to tell.

When we stepped onto the ice, it was like being transported back in time. The cold bit at my cheeks, and the sounds of skates cutting into the ice surrounded us like music. I wobbled at first, my balance off, but Jean's hand was steady in mine, guiding me with gentle confidence. We moved together, slowly at first, but it didn't take long for us to find a rhythm. Every glide, every turn felt like the natural next step, like we were writing a story together with each movement.

Jean's hair floated around her face, catching the light from the overhead lamps, and she looked radiant, more alive than I'd seen her in weeks. I watched her, unable to tear my eyes away, and I could feel the pull of her, that quiet, undeniable gravity that had always drawn me in. She was everything—the calm in the storm, the steady hand that guided me back to myself when I felt lost.

She looked at me, a soft laugh escaping her lips as she pulled me into a gentle spin, and I couldn't help but smile back. We moved in sync, our hands intertwined, our bodies close. I could feel the warmth of her through our layers of coats, the faint scent of her perfume mingling with the crisp, icy air. Every touch, every fleeting brush of her fingers against mine sent a spark through me, reigniting something I'd thought was lost.

We glided past couples holding hands, kids skating clumsily, and we weaved through them effortlessly, like we'd been doing this our whole lives. There was a comfort in it, a quiet understanding that needed no words. I pulled her closer, my arm slipping around her waist as we moved, and she leaned into me, her head resting briefly on my shoulder. My heart swelled, and in that moment, everything else faded away.

As we skated, the world felt sharper, more vivid. I noticed the pink flush in her cheeks and freckled nose, the way her breath fogged in the air when she laughed. I watched the way her eyes sparkled, bright and clear, as she looked up at me, and I couldn't help but wonder how I'd ever let things get so tangled between us.

I wanted to tell her everything—how much I'd missed her,

how lost I'd felt without her, how every second of silence between us had been torture. But the words stuck, trapped behind the flood of emotions that threatened to overwhelm me.

Instead, I held her tighter, letting the movement speak for us. We skated in perfect harmony, each glide and turn feeling like the natural continuation of the last. It was like being part of a story with the perfect plot, with the fullest, most profound characters, and language equal parts delicate and powerful. Every moment felt intentional, every touch deliberate. It was like reading a novel you never wanted to end.

After what felt like both an eternity and no time at all, we slowed, easing off the ice and back onto solid ground. I kept my arm around her, unwilling to let go just yet, and she leaned into me, her breath still coming in soft, ragged puffs. We sat down on the same bench where I'd first spotted her, our skates still on, and I couldn't help but look at her, really look at her, as if I was seeing her for the first time all over again.

"You're incredible," I whispered, my voice hoarse with everything I still couldn't quite say. "You're…you're everything, Jean."

She looked at me, her eyes soft, but there was a hint of something else—something deeper, maybe even a little sad. She reached out, her fingers brushing my cheek, and I leaned into the touch, closing my eyes for a moment just to feel her. "You're not so bad yourself," she said, a hint of a smile tugging at her lips.

I turned my head, pressing a kiss to her palm, and for the first time in days, I felt like we were finally on the same frequency. Whatever had come between us, whatever miscommunications and fears had driven us apart, none of it mattered now. We were here, together, and that was enough.

I pulled her close, wrapping my arms around her as she buried her face in my shoulder. We sat like that for a long time, the sounds of the rink fading into the background, and I hoped that nothing could ever separate us again.

\*\*\*

*Jean*

We stood in front of Edgar Shep's house, a tall, narrow structure that loomed against the sky, its weathered brick facade marked by years of wind, rain, and sun. The house felt impossibly grand and eerily quiet, its windows like dark eyes peering out at the empty street. David stared at it for a long moment, his hands jammed into his coat pockets, his expression unreadable. I glanced up at the three stories, each one stacked neatly on top of the other, and then at the attic window, barely visible at the top like the final chapter of a long and complicated story.

"It always felt too big," David said finally, his voice thick with nostalgia. "Especially after Mom died. It was just me and Dad, rattling around in this huge house. We could go days without really seeing each other, each of us tucked away in our own corners." He laughed bitterly. "We'd pass each other in the hall, say a quick 'good morning' or 'good night,' but that was about it. I used to think it was normal, you know? But looking back, it just feels… sad."

I reached over and squeezed his arm, the fabric of his coat rough against my palm. "You were grieving. Both of you."

David nodded, but the guilt lingered in his eyes. "I should have tried harder. I was too wrapped up in my own world, and he… he was too wrapped up in his."

We stepped inside, the air cold and still, carrying that unmistakable scent of a place that hadn't been lived in for a while—dust and faint hints of old wood and the remnants of a long-ago life. The hallway stretched out before us, narrow and dimly lit, with faded wallpaper and scuffed floors that echoed faintly under our steps. The silence was palpable, broken only by the occasional creak of the house settling around us.

David led the way up the stairs, his movements slow, deliberate, as if each step pulled him further into his memories. We climbed all the way up to the attic, where Edgar had stored the bulk of the family's old things. The room was filled with boxes, some neatly labeled, others stacked haphazardly, as if they'd been abandoned in the midst of some long-forgotten sorting project. Dust particles floated in the streams of light from the small attic window, giving the space an ethereal, almost haunted quality.

David hesitated at the threshold, his gaze sweeping over the cluttered space. "He used to bring me up here sometimes," he said quietly, his voice tinged with a mix of fondness and regret. "We'd look through the old photo albums, dig through stuff from his childhood. But after Mom... I just couldn't. I didn't want to remember."

We spent the next couple of hours going through boxes, sifting through Edgar's life piece by piece. There were old family photos, faded with time but still full of joy, and keepsakes from Edgar's publishing career—framed magazine covers, awards, and letters of thanks from authors whose careers he'd helped shape. Each discovery brought a new wave of emotions, and there were moments when David would stop, his shoulders slumping under the weight of it all.

I kept close to him, gently pulling him back each time the grief threatened to drag him under. "Look at this one," I said, holding up a picture of David as a child, proudly holding up a fish he'd caught, his face beaming with delight. Edgar stood beside him, smiling, a hand resting on his son's shoulder.

David chuckled, wiping at his eyes. "He hated fishing. Only took me because I wanted to go."

I smiled, brushing dust from the edges of the photo. "He loved you."

David nodded, swallowing hard.

We continued, unearthing more treasures—a ticket stub from an old concert Edgar had taken David to, a small figurine from a trip they'd taken to the beach, and more photos that spanned decades. I took each one David set aside to be included with the memorabilia to be displayed at the funeral home. With each photo we arranged, each memory pieced together, I could see the hope returning to David's eyes, little by little.

We found a small box labeled "David's Childhood," tucked away behind a larger crate. Inside were drawings, report cards, and the kinds of trinkets that spoke of a boy's life—action figures, model cars, and a set of plastic army men. David sifted through it all, lost in memories, until he pulled out a folded piece of paper that made him laugh—a hand-drawn birthday card he'd made for his father when he was eight. The drawing was messy, the handwriting barely legible, but the sentiment was clear.

"'To the best dad in the world,'" David read aloud, smiling despite himself. "I was such a little suck-up."

I smiled, leaning against him. "It's sweet."

He pressed the card to his chest for a moment before tucking it back in the box, and for the first time since we'd arrived, I saw a real, genuine smile light up his face. It faded quickly though. "Mom died two years later, and we both changed."

It was the same age I'd been when Beth and her mom came into my small family's life for the first time. Such were the watershed moments.

Once we'd gone through everything, I gathered the photos and memorabilia neatly into an empty box, ready for the tribute video and the memory display. David watched me work, his eyes soft, a quiet gratitude in the way he looked at me.

"Thank you, Jean," he said, his voice low. "I don't know what I'd do without you."

I met his gaze, my heart aching at the sincerity in his words. "You won't have to find out."

After packing up the attic, we made our way to the second floor. David's father's bedroom felt frozen in time, as though Edgar had just stepped out for the work day and would be back any second. The faint scent of his cologne, something woodsy and old-fashioned, still lingered in the air, clinging to the heavy drapes and neatly made bed.

David hesitated at the closet, his fingers grazing the doorknob before pulling it open. Inside, the rows of suits hung like forgotten memories, each one a remnant of Edgar's tall, lean frame. David's breath hitched slightly, his shoulders tense as he rifled through the muted grays and blues, searching for the right one, the one that would make his father look dignified in his final hours above ground.

Tucked away at the far end, like a garish punchline, we found a green velvet suit with bell bottoms. It was hideous—seventies-style, with wide lapels and a mustard-yellow tie hanging from the hanger as if it were still waiting for its grand entrance. David stared at it, brow furrowed, before bursting into laughter that surprised us both.

"Did he think he was in a rock band?" David choked out between laughs, his eyes glistening with a mixture of grief and absurdity. I couldn't help but laugh with him, the sound of it cracking through the heavy silence of the room. "I've never seen him wear this. Not once." He shook his head, still smiling, his fingers brushing the velvet as if expecting it to disintegrate into the past.

It was the kind of suit that made you question everything you thought you knew about a person, like discovering a hidden chapter of their life you'd never been privy to. I imagined Edgar—stern, reserved Edgar—in this monstrosity, and the thought was so ridiculous it almost felt like a gift, a fleeting glimpse of some hidden, wilder side of him that we'd never gotten to see.

We tucked it back in the closet, and our laughter faded as David found the familiar brown suit that was truly Edgar.

"This one," David said softly, his voice steadying as he lifted the brown suit from its place. It was simple and timeless, just like Edgar had been. We laid it out on the bed, smoothing the fabric, inspecting it for stray threads or stains that didn't exist. It was perfect.

"What do I do with the rest of this stuff?" David asked, his voice cracking on the last word, as if he were asking more than just a question about clothes. I looked at him, at his strong, broad shoulders that were so different from his father's wiry frame, and I could see the weight of it all settling on him—the responsibility, the grief, the strange emptiness of a life reduced to fabric and seams and photographs.

Edgar's suits were narrow and elegant, built for a man who never quite filled them out. David, by far contrast, was all muscle and strength, built solidly from the ground up, and none of these clothes would ever fit him. They belonged to a different kind of man.

"Goodwill," I said softly, reaching out to touch his arm. "Most of these are out of fashion even though they suited him. Someone else could use them. Someone who needs a break."

David nodded, staring at the closet full of history that didn't seem to have a place in his life anymore. It was hard, I knew, to think about giving away pieces of his father, but there was also a kind of solace in knowing they could help someone who needed them.

"Maybe some guy who's down on his luck will pick up one of these, and it'll give him a little bit of confidence. A fresh start." David's eyes were distant, thoughtful, and I could see him imagining it, picturing someone else walking around in his father's clothes, living a life Edgar never would. He nodded again, this time with a little more resolve, and together we began the quiet task of sorting through Edgar's things, piece by piece, letting go of what we could while holding tight to the memories that would never fade.

I volunteered to take the chosen suit to the funeral home along with the pictures and memorabilia and then drop off the donated clothing to Goodwill. "It will take a few things off your plate at least."

David gave me a grateful smile as we walked down the hallway. He paused at another bedroom and pushed the door open. I couldn't help but smile at the sight. It was a time capsule of 80s teenage rebellion—walls plastered with posters of hair bands, from Motley Crue to Bon Jovi, Twisted Sister, and Madonna. The room was small, with just enough space for a twin bed covered with a faded plaid bedspread, a desk cluttered with old CDs, and a battered bookshelf filled with tattered paperbacks.

Though it looked like a teenager had walked out and never returned, things were dusted and vacuumed. It seemed as though Edgar had kept the room ready for David had he ever wanted to come home. I wondered if David noticed.

I wandered over to the bookshelf, running my fingers along the spines of the books. "This explains so much about you."

"Yeah?" He leaned against the doorframe, watching me. "Like what?"

I pulled out a worn, dog-eared copy of *The Catcher in the Rye*. Annotations from torn pieces of notebook paper and faded yellow sticky notes stuck out from the pages at all angles. "This, for one. The whole *bildungsroman* and your formative years and such."

He rolled his eyes, but there was a smile tugging at his lips. "I thought I was so deep back then."

"You still are." I smirked. "Just maybe with fewer band posters."

We spent the next few minutes exploring the room, laughing at the remnants of his teenage years—the mix tapes, the crumpled concert flyers, and a journal filled with embarrassingly earnest poetry. David's face turned bright red as I flipped through a few pages, but there was a warmth to the moment, a sense of shared history that made everything feel a little lighter.

After a while, we sat on the edge of his bed, and I couldn't help but feel the closeness between us, the electricity that always seemed to hum whenever we were near each other. The room was small, and the bed even smaller, but in that moment, it felt like the only place in the world that mattered.

David turned to me, his expression softening. "Thanks for doing this with me. I don't think I could've... well, you know."

I nodded, reaching out to touch his hand.

He squeezed my fingers, his touch lingering, and when he looked at me, there was something in his blue eyes that went beyond gratitude. It was deeper, fuller, a connection that had always been there but felt more undeniable now than ever. I leaned in, feeling the warmth of him, the familiar scent of his cologne mixed with the old musk of the room, and before I knew it, we were kissing—slow, deliberate, like we had all the time in the world.

His hands found my waist, pulling me closer, and I could feel the strength of him, the way his touch was both tender and urgent. It was like every unsaid thing between us was spilling out in that moment, every unspoken promise and every quiet longing. We moved together, slow and sure, our bodies fitting together perfectly on that small bed, the past and present colliding in the most beautiful way.

We didn't need to say anything. The way he held me, the way he touched me, was enough. It was a connection that went beyond words, a slow burn that had been kindling for years, finally finding its ignition. The room faded around us—the posters, the clutter, the recent distance, and the miscommunication. All that mattered was us, here, now, in this moment.

David kissed me deeply, his hands trailing down my back, as I tossed our clothing aside, and I felt like I was floating, caught between the boy he used to be and the man he'd become. Every touch was a revelation, every kiss a promise that whatever we were, whatever we were becoming, it was real and it was ours. There was only the two of us, tangled in each other, finding solace in the spaces where we'd once been broken.

When it was over, we lay there, breathless and content, our limbs entwined, and for the first time in a long time, I felt whole. David's fingers traced lazy circles on my back, and I closed my eyes, savoring the warmth of him, the safety of this small, messy room that had once been his world.

"Thank you," he whispered, his voice rough and filled with a tenderness that sent shivers down my spine.

I looked up at him, my heart full. "For what?"

"For being here. For seeing me." He paused, his thumb brushing my cheek. "For making this house feel like home again."

I smiled, pressing my forehead to his, and in that small, sacred space, I knew that whatever came next, we'd face it together. The past was behind us, and the future finally felt like something worth looking forward to.

# Chapter Five

*Beth*

I tapped my fingernails against the kitchen counter, each sharp click a reminder of my growing impatience. The past couple of days had been agonizingly quiet, the silence from David and Jean unsettling. I'd been expecting more opportunities to mess with their lives, to inject myself into their fractured relationship, but my phone had been infuriatingly silent.

No texts from Jean or David meant no way to twist the knife, and I was starting to wonder if they'd figured out my switch of contacts. The thought made my pulse quicken with nervous energy. If they knew, it would all be over. My control over their conversations—their entire perception of each other—would be gone, and with it, my last thread of influence in David's life.

I paced the length of my apartment, biting my lip as I

checked my phone for the hundredth time. I'd made a game out of orchestrating their misunderstandings, crafting replies that were just wrong enough to make them question each other without realizing they were being played. But now, the game was stalling, and I was losing my patience.

Just when I was about to throw my phone down in frustration, it buzzed. A text. My heart leapt as Jean's name appeared on the screen, and I scrambled to read the message:

*You know, you really should have kept that green velvet suit back from the Goodwill donations. I think you should have tried it on sometime. You'd look like the most dapper leprechaun at the party! :-)*

I laughed, though the sound was bitter. The little joking exchanges between them, the kind of light-hearted banter that once would have been mine with David, now twisted in my mind as another reminder of how far I'd been pushed out. I quickly forwarded Jean's message to David's contact, keeping up the pretense that everything was normal between them. Jean's playful words would reach him, but it wasn't enough. I needed more. Something bigger. Something that would dig deep and leave a lasting scar.

Jean's next message was less frivolous:

*I just dropped off the pictures, memorabilia, and clothing for Edgar at the funeral home. The attendants were so kind. They promised to set everything up. I hope it all goes smoothly.*

142

I felt a spark of inspiration flicker inside me, malicious and gleeful. If Jean was helping with the funeral arrangements, that meant she was doing the best she could to support David, playing the role of the perfect girlfriend in his time of need. But what if I could turn her act of kindness into something that would haunt them both? An idea formed, dark and delicious, and I knew exactly what I needed to do.

Without wasting another second, I grabbed my purse and keys, and made my way to my stylist shop. I picked out a red wig that was nearly identical to Jean's red hair—soft curls and waves just a bit untamed—and used my makeup kit to recreate her freckles. As I applied it, carefully dotting the freckles across my cheeks and nose, I studied myself in the mirror. The resemblance was close enough; the oversized sunglasses I'd brought along would hide the differences.

Satisfied, I pulled on a long coat and headed out, my heart racing with anticipation. I drove to the Goodwill in Elmburn, the one closest to David's father's house, and parked at the back entrance. The store was bustling with people dropping off donations and rifling through racks, but I didn't pay them any mind. I went straight to the donation area, where items were piled haphazardly in bins waiting to be sorted. I scanned the heaps of clothes, my breath catching as I recognized several familiar items. A tie I'd seen Edgar wear to some publishing event, a wool coat with a small tear at the sleeve. And then I saw it—the sleeve of a green velvet suit.

No wonder Jean was joking about it. It was hideous, an old-fashioned relic that Edgar had probably worn to some office Christmas party decades ago, but that wasn't the point. I reached for it, my fingers curling around the fabric, and pulled it free from the pile. The color was garish, the material heavy and outdated, but it was perfect. It was the last thing anyone would want Edgar to be remembered in, and the thought of him laid out in this ridiculous suit, with David assuming Jean had somehow caused it—it was too delicious to pass up.

I slipped it into a garment bag I'd brought along, and then hurried away from the store before anyone could question me. My heart pounded with adrenaline as I drove to the funeral home, rehearsing my lines in my head. I pulled up to the front entrance, adjusted my wig and sunglasses, and made my way inside, trying to mimic Jean's skittery, mousey demeanor. The receptionist glanced up, her brow furrowing slightly as I approached.

"Hi there," I said, injecting a slight tremor of nervousness into my voice. "Do you remember me? I was just in here a little bit ago."

She nodded, her expression softening with recognition. "Yes, of course. You dropped off some clothing for Mr. Shep's arrangements."

I offered a tight smile, feeling my pulse race. "Right, but there's been a change. I'm so sorry to be a bother, but I brought this instead." I held up the garment bag, my hand trembling just enough to sell the act. "Is it too late?"

The receptionist glanced at her clipboard, then shook her head. "No, we haven't completed the dressing yet. It's not too late at all. Would you like me to make the switch?"

Relief and triumph washed over me. "Yes, please. Thank you so much for being flexible."

The attendant took the bag from me, and I watched as she disappeared down the hall, my heart swelling with satisfaction. I could already picture the scene: David's face falling as he saw his father dressed in that ridiculous green suit, the one he knew Jean had suggested keeping as a joke. The anger, the hurt, the inevitable blame—it would be more than enough to shatter whatever tentative peace they'd managed to find. And Jean, poor naive Jean, would have no idea how it had happened. She'd think it was her fault, that she'd somehow caused this awful final impression of Edgar, and David would never let her forget it.

I left the funeral home feeling giddy, the thrill of my deception coursing through me. I couldn't wait to see how it all played out, how my small but perfectly calculated act would ripple through their lives. For now, I'd sit back and watch as everything unraveled, knowing that this time, I'd outmaneuvered them both.

As I drove home, I pulled off the red wig and tossed it onto the passenger seat, wiping away the fake freckles that had dotted my face. I felt like I'd won a small but significant victory. David and Jean had been slipping away from my control, their growing closeness threatening to shut me out completely, but now I'd planted the seeds of doubt once again. They'd be left questioning each other, their trust shaken, and I'd be right there to savor every delicious moment of their unraveling.

I couldn't wait to see what happened next.

***

*David*

I walked into the funeral home, my stomach twisted in knots I hadn't felt since the call that started all of this. The sickening scent of lilies hit me first, mingling with the faint, familiar whiff of furniture polish. There were people—so many people already there—huddled in small groups, their voices low and respectful, but their presence only added to the surreal weight of it all. Cousins I hadn't seen in years, aunts and uncles who seemed to have aged overnight, all milling about, shaking hands and exchanging murmured condolences. I managed

146

tight, polite smiles as I moved through the crowd, adjusting the knot in my tie that suddenly seemed to choke me, nodding at familiar faces but keeping my pace brisk.

I couldn't linger; I needed to see him first. I needed to make sure everything was perfect.

The doors to the chapel were closed, but the funeral director, a stocky man with kind eyes and a perpetually worried expression, gestured me in with a nod. "Take your time," he said softly, but I barely heard him.

My focus was already on the space ahead, on the soft, golden light spilling from the stained glass, on the rows of flower arrangements that lined the walls in an elegant display of love and loss. The fragrance was overwhelming, a cloying reminder of all the people who had cared, all the people who had reached out to pay their respects to my father. Even in death, he was surrounded by the signs of a life well-lived, every bouquet and plant a testament to how much he was admired, respected, maybe even loved.

But it all faded as I moved closer to the casket, a deep shiny auburn metal. Despite the scrolling and frills of the hardware, it was still a box for a body. I found I couldn't focus on his profile from a distance. Instead my mind, chucked everything at me that I hadn't said. All the things I'd left undone. Things I had said in the pride of youth, invincible. Things I hadn't really meant but had never bothered to apologize for saying.

My feet carried me even though I didn't want to approach the casket. I froze, breath caught in my throat, staring at the figure lying there in something I could not comprehend. My father, still and serene, was dressed in *the green velvet suit*. The one Jean and I had laughed about, the one that didn't belong in this place, this moment. It was garish, ridiculous, and so far removed from anything I'd imagined when we carefully chose his clothes.

My heart pounded, my blood turning to ice as I stood there, unable to reconcile what I was seeing with what I knew had been decided. The absurdity of it crashed over me in waves—this wasn't just a mistake; it felt like a betrayal. My mind raced, immediately jumping to Jean. *How could she have done this? Why would she do this?*

I turned on my heel and stormed out of the chapel, fury blinding me to the concerned looks of family members who stepped aside as I barreled past. The funeral director was standing nearby, talking to an attendant, but I barely gave him time to finish his sentence before I was in his face.

"Who dressed him?" I demanded, my voice low and trembling with barely contained anger. "He's in the wrong damn suit! He should be in a brown one. Jean dropped it off— red hair, freckles—you couldn't miss her."

"I—I'm sorry, Mr. Shep. Let me check the details." The director's eyes widened as he moved over to a tall counter in an office section. He fumbled with a folder filed on the wall, flipping through notes with fingers that seemed suddenly clumsy. He nodded to the attendant, a young woman with a tense expression, who shuffled nervously next to him.

"Sir," the attendant stammered. "There was one suit dropped off. But then, a couple of hours later, another one was brought in to swap it out. The dressing hadn't been completed yet, so we switched the bags."

My stomach dropped. "Who brought the second suit?" I asked, my voice like gravel.

The attendant hesitated, glancing at the director, who nodded for her to continue. "A woman with red hair," she said. "Just like you described."

It felt like the floor was crumbling beneath me. This had to be some kind of joke, a sick, twisted joke that made no sense. I clenched my fists, trying to steady the whirl of emotions— anger, disbelief, betrayal. I didn't want to believe it. I didn't want to believe that Jean could be capable of something so cruel.

"We have other suits," the director said quickly, his voice desperate to defuse the tension. "We can change him right now. We won't allow anyone else to view him until you've given final approval."

"Do it," I snapped. The staff scattered, moving with urgency, but I was too wrapped up in my own seething anger to care. I stepped back, pacing the hallway, running a hand through my hair as I tried to process it.

Then I saw her—Jean, walking in, clothed in a conservative black dress, nylons, and heels, her expression softening into a concerned smile as she spotted me. But all I saw was red. I grabbed her elbow and pulled her toward the front door, the sudden motion catching her off guard.

"David!" she exclaimed, stumbling slightly as I dragged her outside. "What the hell—what are you doing?"

I released her the moment we were outside, taking a step back and glaring at her, my hands shaking at my sides. "You need to explain yourself," I said, my voice tight with barely controlled fury.

Jean looked at me, her brow furrowing in confusion. "What are you talking about? Explain what?"

"The suit!" I shouted, unable to keep my voice from rising. "My dad is in that goddamn green velvet suit. The one we laughed about. Why would you do that?"

Her eyes widened, genuinely shocked, and for a second, I almost believed she didn't know what I was talking about. "David, I gave them the suit you picked out! The brown one!"

"Then how the hell did he end up in the green one?" I demanded, feeling the heat rising in my chest. "They said someone swapped it out. A woman with red hair."

Jean's face paled. She looked away, biting her lip as she tried to piece together what I was saying. "I didn't swap anything," she said finally, her voice cracking. "You saw me bag up the brown suit yourself. I left it at the desk with the pictures and everything else. I wouldn't—David, I swear, I wouldn't do that!"

"Yeah?" I shot back, my anger spiking again. "Well, they're saying different. You were the only one who was supposed to handle this. You were the one I trusted with this. And now, look at this mess."

She opened her mouth to respond, but nothing came out. I could see the hurt in her eyes, the disbelief that I would think she could do something like this, but I was too angry to care. It all felt too raw, too personal. "If you're going to make a mockery of my father's funeral," I said coldly, "then don't bother showing up. And don't bother coming to the office, either. You're fired."

The words hung in the air between us, heavy and final. Jean's expression shifted, a flash of something breaking behind her eyes, but she didn't speak. She just stood there, her face crumpling into a mix of sorrow and anger, before she turned and walked away without another word. I watched her go, feeling a bitter satisfaction that quickly twisted into something darker, something that made my stomach churn. I had never seen her look so small, so defeated, and it should have felt like some kind of victory. But it didn't. It felt like another loss, piled on top of all the others.

I turned back toward the funeral home, my heart pounding, knowing I would have to go back in there, face my family, and pretend that everything was okay. But nothing was okay. Not anymore.

***

*Jean*

I parked my car in front of the bar, gripping the steering wheel so tightly my hands hurt. David's words still echoed in my mind, biting and unforgiving. *You were the one I trusted with this.* His accusation felt like a slap. The dressing mix-up at the funeral home had to be Beth's doing, a cruel joke meant to come between us. How she managed it, I didn't know, but it was exactly like her to pull something so terrible. So underhanded. But David hadn't seen that. He'd only seen me, he'd seen a problem, and he hadn't considered any other possibilities.

I squeezed my eyes shut, trying to block it all out. I got out of my vehicle and walked slowly toward the entrance. The heavy smell of stale cigarettes and cheap beer drifted from the bar, and I thought about losing myself in the noise and the alcohol, drowning the hurt away. But just as I reached for the door handle, my phone buzzed. It was Frederick:

*Staying in town for a couple more days. Up for a late-night adventure?*

I stared at the screen, the words blurring together. Frederick Donelson was the last person I should be thinking about tonight. He was dangerous in his own way, a charming, intoxicating distraction from everything I was struggling to hold together. But the thought of David's scorn, his refusal to let me attend his father's funeral, his firing me, all weighed heavy. I needed to forget, even if just for a few hours.

*I'm in a difficult spot tonight. I need fun. Just fun. No mistakes.*

I hit send before I could second-guess myself, my heart hammering against my ribs. Frederick was trouble, the kind that made you feel alive but also made you question everything. And right now, maybe that's exactly what I needed.

I received his response in seconds: *Agreed. Where can we meet?*

Twenty minutes later, I pulled into the parking lot of a 24/7 diner that I knew was about halfway between his hotel and the bar I had stopped at. Frederick was already there, leaning casually against a sleek, matte gun-metal Lamborghini underlit by stunning red lights. He stood like a vision pulled straight from a magazine, dressed in tight black jeans that clung to his long, lean legs and a soft gray button-up shirt that fit him just right, accentuating his broad chest and flat stomach. Over it, he wore a leather jacket, the kind that aged gracefully, holding stories in its creases. The streetlights caught the faint glimmer of the jacket's worn edges, adding to the aura of effortless cool that radiated from him.

He looked dangerous, carefree, untamed. And the devil-may-care grin on his face only served to send a shiver of attraction down my spine. As he glanced over at me, his eyes lit up in a way that made my stomach flip. He exuded a magnetic pull that was impossible to ignore.

"You know, you don't have to pretend to be okay if you're not," he said, offering me a small, knowing smile as I stepped out of my vehicle.

I shrugged, stuffing my hands into my coat pockets. "I'm not okay. But I also don't want to complicate things any further than they already are. And you could be a complication…a dangerous one in that jacket and with this car." I couldn't help but grin.

He laughed, a warm, genuine sound that cut through the chill of the night. "I won't deny that. But let's keep it light and have some fun. No pressure, no strings. Just… something good."

I hesitated, but his smile was disarming, and right now, a little bit of good was all I wanted. "What do you have in mind?"

He gestured to the Lamborghini, gleaming under the streetlights. "How about a ride?"

He pressed a button on the fob in his hand, and the scissor doors opened with a soft hiss, revealing an interior that was so pristine that it felt almost sacred.

"How in the world did you find something like this in Elmburn?" I asked, peeking into the immaculate black leather interior with red stitching. There was something recklessly exhilarating about it.

"A friend of a friend."

"Well, maybe you should introduce me to some of these friends," I laughed.

He chuckled as I slid down onto the seat, my heart skipping a beat as I ran my fingers along the smooth leather that was perfectly heated. The small, luxurious space felt like slipping into a secret world—cocooned in warmth, surrounded by the quiet hum of power waiting to be unleashed. Frederick joined me, his presence filling the car.

We shot off into the night, the car leaping onto the road, born to race, the wind whipping by as the city blurred into streaks of neon and shadows. I held on tight, feeling every turn and curve in the road, the force of the speed pinning me back as the thrill of it tingled through my veins. I couldn't help but laugh—giddy, breathless, and utterly alive.

Frederick took sharp corners without hesitation, expertly weaving through the empty streets, and the noise in my head finally quieted. My pulse raced with each twist, perfectly controlled yet on the edge of chaos, and every worry, every lingering doubt faded into nothingness. In this moment, with Frederick beside me and the world rushing past, I felt invincible, swept up in the reckless, intoxicating freedom of the night.

We pulled up to an all-night winter carnival on the southeast end of the city that was in full swing, the kind with glowing ice sculptures, snow-dusted paths, and the comforting scents of hot cocoa and spiced apple cider filling the crisp night air. It was like stepping into another world, one where my problems didn't exist and fun was the only goal.

Frederick parked, and we strolled through the snowy grounds, taking in the sights. The carnival was more crowded than I expected for such a late hour, filled with a mixture of families, couples, and stragglers who seemed to drift between booths as aimlessly as we did. The sounds of laughter, the soft crunch of snow underfoot, and the faint, haunting melody of a wind chime made of icicles filled the air, blending into a magical winter symphony that felt like stepping into another world.

Frederick and I wandered along the rows of booths, snowflakes swirling around us under the soft glow of string lights. The carnival was decorated with intricate ice sculptures, frozen in lifelike poses, and snowmen with carrot noses and scarves that seemed to smile at us as we passed. There was an understanding between us tonight—a pact to keep things light, even though there were moments when something heavier threatened to seep through.

We stopped at a snowball throwing game. Frederick picked up one of the snowballs, compacting it between his gloved hands with ease.

"Think you've got this?" I teased, arching an eyebrow.

Frederick smirked, giving the snowball a playful toss up. "Always. But let's see what you've got first."

I squared my shoulders, taking the snowball from him. The targets were painted snowmen faces, waiting to be knocked over. I threw the first snowball, which veered slightly off course and only grazed the side of the target. Frederick laughed softly, not unkindly, and took his turn. His throw was perfect, sending the snowman head tumbling down with a satisfying thud.

"Show-off," I muttered, but there was no real heat behind it. He handed me the next snowball, guiding my hand with his own, and I could feel the warmth of his touch even through our gloves. My heart fluttered, and I looked up at him, our faces just inches apart. His expression was serious, focused, but there was a flicker of something more in his eyes.

"Try again," he said softly.

I took a deep breath, steadying myself before I threw. This time, the snowball hit dead center, knocking the target over in one clean shot. I whooped in triumph, and Frederick lifted his hands in mock surrender.

"Alright, alright. I admit it—you're better than I gave you credit for."

I couldn't help but laugh, the tension between us momentarily forgotten. "Well, I better be, or my brother would never forgive me."

"Does he play ball?" Frederick asked.

"He used to. Maybe you've heard of him. George Price?" I said it nonchalantly, already knowing what reaction I would get—even from someone like Frederick Donelson.

He stood frozen. "The George Price. Your brother is George Price? Of the Elmburn Blues? MVP? World Series, George freaking Price?"

"Mmhmm." I grazed the edge of his open jaw with my index finger. "Oh, come on. Like he's a big deal to someone like you?" I teased and turned away, pretending to be interested in the next snowball game.

"Um, yes!"

I laughed, and he caught me by the waist, spinning me around, which brought more laughter from me. I rested my hands against his chest, reveling in the grin on his face. My heart beat faster. He swallowed hard and released me. I recognized the look in his eyes as a mixture of longing and resignation because I felt the same.

"Seriously though," he said as we moved on to a booth offering steaming cups of cocoa and cider, along with handmade trinkets and small plush toys. "Think I could get his autograph?"

I laughed again. "Absolutely. I'll introduce you sometime."

We kept walking, my feet leading me toward a tent draped in dark, tattered fabric and dimly lit by strings of flickering bulbs. A hand-painted sign swung above the entrance: *Madame Verda's Tarot Readings – See Your Future Revealed!* I hesitated, drawn to the tent almost against my will.

"Want to have your fortune told?" Frederick asked, reading the curiosity in my expression.

I shrugged. "Why not? I could use some good news."

The inside of the tent smelled of incense, and the air was thick and heavy, filled with a mysterious energy that made the hairs on the back of my neck stand up. At a small, round table sat an older woman, her face lined with age and framed by a cascade of wild, silver hair. She wore layers of brightly colored scarves, and her light eyes ice-blue eyes were unnervingly piercing.

"Sit," she said, gesturing to the chair opposite her. "Let Madame Verda see what lies ahead."

Frederick tossed a couple of bills into the woman's basket and leaned against the tent's pole beside where I sat, watching with a half-smile. I sat down, suddenly feeling more vulnerable than I expected. The tarot reader shuffled her cards, each one worn and weathered, and began to lay them out in a deliberate, careful pattern.

She flipped over the first card—a woman standing between two pillars, holding a scroll in her hands.

"The High Priestess," Madame Verda said, her voice a low murmur. "You are at a crossroads, torn between paths. One of wisdom, the other of desire."

I glanced at Frederick, feeling a strange chill run through me. The reader continued, revealing more cards—The Lovers, The Tower, and The Three of Swords.

"You stand in the center of a love triangle," she said, her eyes flicking up to meet mine. "Two paths diverge, each leading to different futures. One is stable, rooted in the past. The other is wild, unpredictable, and new."

I bit my lip, unable to tear my gaze away from the cards. "Who wins out?"

Madame Verda stared at the cards for a long moment before looking back at me. "Neither," she said cryptically. "You'll find yourself marooned on an island, alone with your true love. But which man you bring with you is a choice only you can make."

*True love isn't a choice*, I told myself. *Is it?*

Her words hung in the air, heavy and uncertain. My mind spun, trying to decipher the meaning, but all I could see was the image of David and Frederick, their faces blurred together in a confusing mix of loyalty and longing.

Frederick rested his hand gently on my shoulder. He chuckled softly, but his eyes were serious. "I think she's just trying to get in your head," he whispered as he leaned in close.

Maybe he was right. Maybe it was just a game, a bit of carnival mystique meant to dazzle and distract. But it was hard to shake the feeling that Madame Verda had seen something real, something I wasn't ready to confront.

As we wandered further into the carnival, we found ourselves drawn to the carousel, its lights glowing against the dark night. I climbed onto one of the horses, the paint chipped and faded, but still beautiful in that nostalgic way only old carnival rides could be. Frederick took the horse beside mine, and as the ride began to turn, I felt the gentle up-and-down motion carry away the last of my anxieties.

"This is kind of ridiculous, isn't it?" I said, laughing as my horse bobbed in time to the tinny music. My breath puffed in cold clouds. "I feel like I'm five years old."

Frederick watched me, his smile softening into something more genuine. "I think it's perfect."

We rode in comfortable silence, the world spinning slowly around us. The carnival lights blurred and reflected off the nearby ice sculptures of mythical animals, and for a moment, it was just the two of us, lost in the simplicity of the night. When the carousel finally stopped, Frederick helped me down, his hand lingering on mine just a little longer than necessary. I didn't pull away.

"I'm glad you texted me," I said, breaking the silence. "I needed tonight."

"Me too," he replied, his voice tinged with a kind of quiet sincerity that I hadn't expected.

The night was slipping away faster than I wanted, and as we made our way back to the car, Frederick suddenly turned to me, a mischievous glint in his eyes. "One more stop."

I gave him a skeptical look. "Where?"

He grinned. "Trust me."

The engine roared to life, vibrating through my body. We sped off into the night, the city blurring into streaks of neon lights and shadows.

The city around us was alive with flickering street lamps,

late-night diners, and the occasional buzz of a distant siren. We sliced through narrow alleys and zipped past sleepy storefronts.

Frederick took sharp turns without hesitation, a thrill building in my chest that matched the reckless pace he set. We finally skidded to a stop at the base of the tallest building I'd ever seen up close—a forgotten tower that pierced the skyline, its upper floors swallowed in darkness.

I stared up at it when Frederick sprung the doors. He came over to my side with a grin, taking my hand and tugging me gently from the warmth of the vehicle. Then we slipped inside the building through a series of half-hidden entrances: a rusted side door, a forgotten service stairwell, and narrow passages that twisted through the building's guts. We ducked behind walls, flattened against alcoves, and stilled our breaths as we narrowly missed security guards, maintenance workers, and a couple sneaking a smoke on the twenty-fourth floor.

My heart pounded with each story we climbed, the thrill of sneaking through the maze-like structure sending adrenaline coursing through my veins. The eightieth floor and above were clearly marked as closed, but we still continued. As we reached the final stairwell on the ninety-second floor, the steps creaked under our weight. My legs burned, but Frederick's determined grip pulled me forward.

Finally, we reached the roof access door and pushed

through, greeted by the crisp night air and the dazzling sprawl of Elmburn beneath us. The city glittered in every direction, a sea of lights reflecting off the river and skyscrapers standing like silent sentinels.

I turned to Frederick, breathless and awed. "How did you know your way?"

He chuckled, a soft, triumphant sound that cut through the wind. "I didn't. I was making it up as we went. Saw this building from my flight earlier this week and decided I needed to see Elmburn from the top."

We stood side by side, the rush of the city below our feet, feeling like the only two souls on top of the world.

"This is...something," I said, my voice barely above a whisper.

Frederick leaned against the railing, his gaze soft as he watched me. "I figured you could use the perspective."

The weight of everything hit me all at once. I leaned against the railing, my fingers gripping the cold metal. I turned an idea over in my mind. Should this go any further in the future with Frederick, he should know me fully. There would be no hiding or pretending with him. "Would you be my sounding board?"

He nodded.

"I've been in love with my boss for six years."

Frederick crossed his arms over his broad chest. "David

Shep?"

I nodded. "It's been especially complicated this last year because he's been in a relationship with my step-sister, Beth. They got engaged recently, but she broke it off."

I took a deep breath. "David and I sort of hit things off right after, but the timing is horrible because his father just died, and we've had one misunderstanding after the next. The worst was earlier tonight."

I explained the clothing mistake at the funeral home. Frederick listened intently.

"David thinks I did it on purpose. I know it was Beth somehow. I would never do that. I loved Edgar Shep."

Frederick's expression didn't change, but his eyes darkened, thoughtful. "And what was David's reaction?"

"He told me not to come to the funeral tomorrow, and…" I paused, still unable to believe it myself. "He fired me."

Frederick was silent for a moment, letting my words hang between us. "David's an idiot if he can't see that you wouldn't do something like that."

I swallowed hard, my throat tight. "I've loved him for so long, Frederick. And tonight, he just looked at me like I was nothing but a cruel monster."

Frederick moved toward me at the railing, not touching but close enough that I felt his warmth. "Jean, even in the short time

I've known you, I know that is impossible. You're fire and grit and…God, you're more than most people could handle."

I blinked back the sting of tears, trying to hold myself together. "I'm tired of fighting for someone who doesn't see me."

He nodded, understanding without needing to say much. "Sometimes it's not about being seen by the people who don't get you. Sometimes, it's about being seen by the ones who do. And if a man can't see how amazing you are, he doesn't deserve you."

I turned to look at him, really look at him, and the air between us felt charged, thick with unspoken words. He wasn't pushing, wasn't demanding anything from me. He was just there, steady and solid, the kind of presence that felt grounding in a world that was suddenly constantly shifting beneath my feet.

"I was right about you being trouble." I said, my voice wavering between a laugh and a sigh.

Frederick smiled, his eyes bright and earnest. "Maybe. But I'd rather be trouble than nothing at all to you."

I laughed, a soft, broken sound that came from somewhere deep. "I'm not sure what I want right now. Everything's a mess."

"Then don't decide tonight," he said gently. "Just be here.

Let it be simple."

We stood there, side by side, watching the city below. It would have been so easy to close the distance, to lean in and let the night take us somewhere dangerous and thrilling. But we didn't. Instead, we just stayed in that moment, the quiet and the comfort enough to get me through.

Frederick's words echoed in my mind as we finally headed back down the building's abandoned upper floors, and as he returned me to my vehicle at the diner.

As he opened my door for me, he paused, his expression serious. "Be good to yourself, Jean. Whatever happens with David, remember that you deserve more than someone who makes you question your worth."

I nodded, touched by his sincerity. "Thank you. For tonight. For…everything."

He smiled, but there was something sad in it, like he knew this was all we could have right now. "Anytime, Jean."

We said our goodbyes, lingering a second longer than necessary, both of us aware of the unspoken pull between us. And as I drove away, the city lights reflecting in my rearview mirror, I felt a strange mix of hope and heartbreak.

Tonight was exactly what I needed—a reminder that there was still something good out there, something fun, something that wasn't a struggle and that didn't have to hurt.

# Chapter Six

*Jean*

My phone was ringing. I rolled over reaching for it, and managed to tug it off the charger. Bleary-eyed, I swiped, held it up to my ear, and spoke through my sleeplessness.

"Hello?"

*Beep beep beep.* The line cut out as the caller disconnected.

"Shit." I squinted at my phone, lowered the brightness and went into my recent call list. David. He'd called three times in the last half hour.

Quickly, I tapped his name and called him back. After one ring, my call was sent to voicemail. I didn't even get to hear his recorded voice on the greeting. Instead, the standard robotic-voice track began to drone. When did he change that?

I hit the end button a couple of seconds in, and set my phone down on my chest, swallowing hard. It was barely six o'clock in the morning. I'd finally fallen asleep a little after four. The emotional high I'd garnered with Frederick hadn't lasted long once I'd gotten home alone, and the wheels in my brain started whirring on the same repeated tracks.

My phone beeped with a text from David:

*Can't talk right now but need a favor.*

I drew in a deep breath through my nose. A favor. Jackass. I wouldn't spend one more minute pining over him.

My thumbs stabbed the keyboard: *A favor? You have a lot of nerve asking me for anything.*

*Please Jean. Don't do this right now. I REALLY NEED a favor.*

I hesitated in responding, and he sent another message:

*For Dad's funeral.*

I stared at my phone, David's message glaring back at me like a challenge. After everything—after the shouting, the accusations, and him firing me—he still had the nerve to ask for my help. Part of me wanted to turn my phone off, let him figure out whatever mess he was drowning in on his own. It was too soon, the argument still raw, his voice echoing in my mind: *You're fired.* I tightened my grip, feeling the anger surge again.

All because of that damn suit. Beth was always pulling the strings from behind the scenes. If I had just done something sooner about my feelings for David, maybe none of this would have happened.

But David? Did he deserve my help—after the way he'd reacted? And yet, no matter how much I tried to harden my heart, Edgar's voice kept slipping through, reminding me of every lesson, every moment he'd been there when I needed someone. I hated what David had done, but I couldn't hate Edgar.

I let out a long, shaky breath, my thumbs hovering over the screen. I still loved Edgar, despite the mess we were in now. He'd been more than a mentor; he'd been a lifeline when I was lost, someone who saw something in me when no one else did, not even myself. I couldn't count how many times he'd sat me down with a cup of coffee and given me the advice I didn't even know I needed. He'd believed in me, and I couldn't just walk away from that. Not even now.

I didn't owe David a damn thing, but I owed Edgar everything. And I had to acknowledge that I still loved David. And if helping him meant honoring Edgar's memory, then I'd have to put my pride aside, just this once.

My chest tightened with all the things left unsaid, all the ways I wished I could rewind and fix what was broken. But maybe helping now was my way of making it right, or at least starting to. With a heavy sigh, I finally typed out a reply, my fingers trembling as I hit send, committing to something I wasn't sure I could handle but knew I had to do:

*What do you need?*

*The casket spray is completely wrong. I need you to go to Shipley's Floral and get the replacement. They said they can't get here before the service. I need you to bring it to the funeral home.*

I hesitated to respond again. I knew Shipley's Floral was located about as far away from the funeral home and church as you could get. The funeral was scheduled for 9 o'clock. Even if the roads were good, which I doubted from the dreary look of a winter storm outside my bedroom window, I would be cutting it close.

*Please Jean.*

I sighed and texted back, *Fine. I will be there as soon as I can.* I rolled out of bed and steadied myself on the dresser as I stood. It was going to be a long day. I would not show up looking like a slob. I threw on a black dress and gathered my hair up high. I applied minimal makeup and pulled black nylons up as fast as I dared, trying not to rip them. Shoving my arms into my winter coat and feet into my boots, I grabbed some strappy high heels to carry along and change into should David choose to apologize when I arrived and allow me to attend the funeral.

Sure enough, morning snow in the last few hours had left the roads slick, a thin sheen of ice hidden beneath layers of powder, as if daring me to make the drive. The biting cold wind stung my cheeks as I scraped the windshield clean, my anger simmering under the surface.

I had replayed every heated word from our argument like a loop I couldn't shut off. Now, though, I couldn't help but feel the tiniest flicker of hope. Maybe this meant David was beginning to realize I wasn't to blame for the suit mix-up at the funeral home. Maybe he realized it was Beth's scheme all along. If so, why hadn't he apologized? Or maybe he just didn't care, and I was still his errand girl even when I wasn't on his payroll.

I could almost hear Edgar's voice in my head, urging me to let it go, to do what was right and not let David's stubbornness get the better of me. But it was hard—so damn hard—to keep driving when every thought and turn felt like an ice patch waiting to spin me out of control.

By the time I reached the floral shop, tucked far away in Gilcrest, a distant suburb of Elmburn, I was exhausted. My nerves were frayed and my hands ached from gripping the wheel too tight.

I pushed open the door to the floral shop, the bell above the door jingling softly as I stepped inside. Warm, humid air hit me like a wall, a sharp contrast to the biting cold outside. The shop was cozy, packed with colorful blooms, potted plants, and the faint, earthy smell of soil and stems. But my eyes were drawn immediately to the casket spray on the counter—bright and cheerful, full of chamomile, chrysanthemums, gerberas, and dahlias. My heart sank. Every single flower was from the daisy family, and I was allergic to all of them.

The florist, an older man with a kind face and a green apron stained from years of working with flowers, looked up from behind the counter. "You must be here for the replacement spray," he said, nodding toward the arrangement. "We just finished it."

I tried to smile, but it felt tight and forced. "This is it?" I asked, my voice edged with disbelief. "Are you sure this is the right one?"

He looked at me, then at the order form in his hand. "Yep, this is the reorder. Said they wanted something cheerful and bright for the service."

"Cheerful and bright," I repeated, trying to keep the frustration out of my tone. "I don't suppose there's anything else that doesn't come with a side of hives?"

The florist gave me a confused look. "I'm sorry. We're a bit backed up, and this is what was ordered."

I sighed, feeling the familiar itch start in my nose. "Perfect," I said, my voice dripping with sarcasm and my nose beginning to drip with snot. "Let's get it loaded, then."

The florist eyed me warily. "You sure you're alright? You look a bit...sensitive to these."

I gave a half-hearted laugh, wiping my nose with the sleeve

of my coat. "Oh, I'm definitely sensitive, but it's fine. It's for Edgar." My voice caught on his name, and I swallowed hard, fighting back the emotion that bubbled up when I thought about him.

"Let me help you carry it to the car," he said, and I followed him outside, each step making my head throb a little more. He carefully lifted the casket spray, sliding it into the back of my crossover. As I reached to adjust the edges, the pollen hit me like a punch, and I was overtaken by a sneezing fit. My eyes watered as I knocked a few chamomile blooms out of place. The florist quickly stepped in, rearranging them with the speed of someone who'd done this a thousand times.

"Are you sure you're going to be okay?" he asked, sounding genuinely worried. He handed me a handkerchief. "The funeral home's a good half-hour drive from here."

I blew my nose loudly, trying to catch my breath. "I'll be fine," I said, though it sounded more like a wheeze. "Just not the ideal commute, but it's…whatever."

Five sneezes ripped through me, fast and hard, making the florist jump. He quickly closed the SUV's hatch, as if sealing off the allergens would do me any good. "Good luck," he said, retreating to the safety of his shop with a worried wave.

"Thanks," I mumbled, wiping my nose again. I slid into the driver's seat, eyes red, head pounding, and started the engine.

The smell of flowers clung to everything, making it impossible to escape. I cranked down the windows, desperate for fresh air, and turned up the radio, trying to drown out the endless loop of doubts running through my mind.

I took a large dose of antihistamines from my purse. *Just get the casket spray delivered*, I told myself. *Then find David. And then…talk.* Because we needed to, whether he wanted to or not. I had to know if this was something we could get through or if everything was over. Everything—my career at Shep and Son I worked hard to build, this new relationship with David that I had been so eager to start after so long. Was that really everything? My dedication to work had been my life for so many years that I started to take stock of what else I had, and I found the results sorely lacking.

I gripped the wheel, determined to get through this drive without falling apart, no matter how much it hurt. I cranked the music louder, trying to drown out the chaos in my head, but every breath was a reminder of what I had lost, and what I was still losing.

The phone rang, and Frederick Donelson's name flashed on the screen. I hit the button on the steering wheel to accept the call, half paying attention as I rolled to a stop at a four-way.

"This is Jean," I said, my voice scratchy, barely a wisp. But before I could even register his response, a sudden, violent jolt sent me lurching forward, my seat belt locking tight against my chest.

The casket spray exploded around me—heavy dahlia and chrysanthemums, bright gerberas bursting into a kaleidoscope of petals, shedding in slow motion as I tried to catch my breath. My vision blurred, the world tilting sideways, and when I looked in the rearview mirror, I saw the twisted metal of my vehicle's rear hatch crumpled like a piece of tin foil.

"Are you okay?" A stranger's voice broke through the haze as my door was flung open. I blinked hard, trying to focus, but all I saw was Elvis Presley standing there—sideburns, white jumpsuit, cape fluttering in the breeze. It was surreal, and the absurdity of it all made me laugh, a high, uncontrollable giggle mixed with sneezes that shook my whole body.

"Are you hurt?" Elvis asked, pulling off his sunglasses to reveal a surprisingly normal, concerned face. I tried to answer, but the words tangled in my throat as I struggled with the seat belt, my fingers clumsy and weak. He reached in, helping me unfasten it, and I stumbled forward, still laughing, unable to stop. I was a mess—sneezing, crying, petals stuck in my hair—and Elvis Presley guided me to the curb, urging me to sit.

I wheezed, trying to wipe my nose on my sleeve as I glanced around. A huge black cargo van that had rear-ended me sat just a few feet away, plastered with a giant, glittering image of Elvis performing. The words ELVIS HAS LEFT THE BUILDING AND IS ON THE ROAD! PERFORMING IN A CITY NEAR YOU! scrolled beneath it, a ridiculous punchline to a day that was already beyond saving.

"Oh, thank God," I mumbled, rubbing my eyes as I tried to piece together what had just happened. "I'm not dead. No offense, Elvis, but you're not exactly the King I was hoping to see when I die."

"Maybe you should sit down," Elvis said, his grip firm but gentle as he guided me to the sidewalk. I collapsed onto the cold, hard surface, feeling the weight of exhaustion, allergies, and sheer disbelief pressing down on me.

"I'm calling an ambulance. Just to have you checked out." He was already dialing, but his voice faded in and out, lost in the ringing that throbbed in my ears.

I saw his lips move, heard the faint buzz of his conversation with the dispatcher, but it all felt far away, like a bad dream I couldn't wake up from.

A car door slammed, and through the fog, I thought I heard my name. I wanted it to be David, coming to find me, but I knew it wasn't. He was too busy somewhere else, probably still tangled up in Beth's lies and his own grief. It was crazy, but for a split second, I convinced myself he was trapped inside my phone, a text message I'd never open, a call I'd never hear.

Everything blurred, the edges of my vision going dark, and then, mercifully, nothing.

***

David

The church was filled with a somber silence as I stood at the entrance, staring at my father's casket. It was draped with a beautiful pall—a heavy, rich cream fabric embroidered with gold and silver threads that shimmered faintly under the muted lights of the sanctuary. The ornate design seemed almost too extravagant for the moment, and yet, it somehow matched the dignity my father had always carried with him. The casket bearers stood at the ready split on either, side of the aisle, their faces set in expressions of quiet respect.

I hesitated, taking in the sight of the casket, the finality of it all suddenly hitting me like a punch to the gut. This was it. The end of my father's journey here, and the beginning of new realities for both of us that I hadn't prepared myself for. The priest said a few words of blessing, his voice echoing off the high ceilings, and I felt the weight of it all settle onto my shoulders. It felt impossible to move, but somehow, I took that first step, following close behind as the casket was slowly wheeled down the aisle.

Every step felt like it was dragging me deeper into a fog. The church was packed—friends, family, people whose faces I vaguely recognized but couldn't place in the moment. The air was thick with the sweet scent of flowers, their blooms arranged in towering displays all around the altar. Roses, lilies, and orchids in a riot of colors formed a stunning backdrop that contrasted sharply with the heavy atmosphere. It was beautiful in a way that felt almost cruel, the bright colors mocking the grief that twisted in my chest.

I found my seat in the front pew, right next to my Aunt Mabel. She clutched a handkerchief tightly in her hand, dabbing at her eyes, her expression stoic but fragile. The priest continued the service, his words blending into a blur of prayers and hymns. I tried to focus, to listen, but my mind kept wandering back to the night before, to Jean. I couldn't shake the look on her face when I'd confronted her about the mix-up with my father's suit. Her hurt, her confusion—it had been so real, so raw, and yet, I'd ignored it all, convinced that she was somehow to blame.

I should've known better because I knew Jean. But in my grief, in my anger, I'd only seen with blinders on, and I'd lashed out at the one person who'd been trying to help me. It was easier to direct my pain somewhere, anywhere, and Jean had been the easiest target.

The funeral went on, each moment stretching out like an eternity. I watched as people approached the casket during communion, placing their hands on it, whispering their final goodbyes. I couldn't bring myself to do the same. I just sat there, staring at the glimmering pall, feeling the loss hit me in waves.

When the time came to carry the casket out, I decided to step in with the casket bearers. I could feel the weight of it through the fabric of my gloves, the heaviness a physical reminder of everything I was losing. We carried it slowly, carefully, out of the church and into the waiting hearse. I climbed into the car behind it, Aunt Mabel beside me, her eyes fixed on the hearse as if she couldn't bear to look away.

The drive to the cemetery was quiet. The procession moved slowly through the city, cars pulling over to the side in a show of respect. I stared out the window, watching the familiar streets pass by, each one holding memories of my father. Everywhere I looked, I saw him—sitting at the café on the corner, shopping downtown, talking to the local bookshops, walking me to school when I was a kid, waving to the neighbors as he mowed the lawn. I'd never realized how much of him was woven into the fabric of this city, and now, with every turn, it felt like the city was slowly unraveling around me.

We reached the cemetery, the long line of cars snaking through the wrought iron gates and up the plowed winding path to the burial site. The sun hung low in the sky, casting long shadows over the rows of headstones poking through snowy knolls. I stepped out of the car, feeling the chill of the afternoon breeze cut through my suit. The casket bearers assembled once more, and together, we lifted the casket and carried it to the grave.

I stood at the edge, my hands clasped in front of me, watching as they lowered my father into the ground. The sound of the straps unwinding was harsh in the quiet, and when the casket settled at the bottom, it felt like the last tether holding me together had been cut. The priest said a final prayer, and one by one, people began to toss handfuls of dirt into the grave, the high ring of earth against metal sending a shiver through me.

I felt so alone. Even surrounded by family, friends, all these people who'd come to pay their respects, I'd never felt more isolated. I kept thinking of Jean—of how she should have been here, standing by my side. Instead, she was hurt and angry because of me. I'd wanted to call her all morning, to apologize, to tell her that I'd been wrong, that I needed her. But I couldn't bring myself to reach for my phone. What was I supposed to say? I'd let my grief and my anger blind me, and now I was paying the price.

I lingered at the graveside longer than most, until finally, the cemetery workers began to fill the grave. I forced myself to turn away, to start the slow walk back to the car, every step feeling heavier than the last.

Back at the funeral home, the reception was in full swing, but the food and the quiet hum of conversation did little to lift the weight pressing down on my chest. I moved through the crowd in a daze, accepting condolences and handshakes with a polite nod, but not really hearing the words. The flowers here were just as beautiful—elegant arrangements set up on every table, each one more elaborate than the last.

I sat down with a glass of water, staring into it like it might hold some answer to the mess I'd made. I couldn't stop replaying the argument with Jean, the way I'd accused her without a second thought. Of all the people in my life, she was the one I trusted most. So why had I been so quick to doubt her?

The thought nagged at me until I heard someone clearing his throat. I looked up to see one of the funeral directors standing before me, the older man who'd been in charge of the service earlier. His expression was cautious.

"Mr. Shep," he began hesitantly. "I wanted to offer my condolences and also to mention something about the, uh, incident with the suit."

I tensed, the knot in my stomach tightening. "Go on."

The director exchanged a quick glance with the female attendant, who'd joined him. "We've been discussing the mix-up, and one of our attendants recognizes the shoes of the woman who brought in the incorrect suit. It's been bothering her all day because she is certain they were unique...very expensive, very specific."

"What are you trying to say?" I asked, my voice low.

The attendant looked over my shoulder, her eyes narrowing slightly. "The woman who brought the wrong suit in is wearing those same shoes today, but she is not a redhead. She must have been wearing a wig yesterday."

I followed her gaze, my blood turning to ice when I saw whom she was looking at. *Beth*. She was across the room, chatting and laughing like this was some kind of social event rather than my father's funeral reception. The bile rose in my throat as the pieces clicked together. It had been her. Of course, it had been her.

I took a step around the funeral director and took a good look at her shoes. At least four-inch heels, they were a vision of artful craftsmanship, but they were definitely expensive, as the attendant stated. The pale pink champagne fabric was rich and luxurious, adorned with delicate silver vines that curled and twisted gracefully across the surface like creeping ivy. Each vine, meticulously detailed, climbed up toward the heel, which was a masterpiece in itself—a sculpted silver creation resembling the stem of a flourishing plant, with its leaves gracefully wrapping around the slender stiletto.

Jean wouldn't be caught dead in anything like them, even

at a funeral. Anger surged through me, hot and unforgiving. Barely aware of what I was doing, I crossed the room in long, quick strides. I stopped just short of Beth, my voice low but sharp.

"You did it, didn't you?" I said, cutting through the chatter around us. "You swapped out my father's suit, and you made sure I would blame Jean."

Beth turned, her expression sliding from faux sympathy to something colder, more calculating. "David, this really isn't the time—"

"No," I snapped, my voice rising. "You made it the time when you pulled this stunt. What kind of sick game are you playing?"

The room had gone quiet, all eyes now on us. Beth's smug smile slipped as she realized there was no scheming her way out of this one. "I don't know what you're talking about," she said, but the tremor in her voice betrayed her.

"You knew exactly what you were doing," I continued, not caring who was watching. "You've been trying to drive a wedge between Jean and me ever since you and I first got together, but this—this was low, even for you."

Beth's face flushed with anger, her composure crumbling. "I was just trying to help, David! Jean doesn't belong here, and you know it. She's been a distraction, a liability—"

"Jean has been nothing but good to me," I said, my voice cracking under the weight of everything I was feeling. "She's been patient, kind, understanding—everything you're not. And I let you turn me against her. I let you make me doubt her, and now—" I shook my head, unable to finish. The words choked me, my throat tight with regret.

Beth's defiance wavered, and for a moment, she looked small, almost pathetic. "I was just trying to protect you," she whispered, but the apology rang hollow.

"Protect me from what? From someone who actually cares about me?" I said, my voice breaking. "Get out, Beth. Leave. We are completely through. I don't ever want to see you again."

She stared at me, stunned, before she grabbed her purse and stormed out, her heels clicking loudly on the tiled floor. The room stayed silent for a beat longer, then people slowly resumed their conversations, pretending they hadn't just witnessed the whole ugly scene.

I stood there, feeling more drained than ever. But amidst the exhaustion, there was also a strange, small sense of relief. I'd finally confronted Beth, and it was over. I didn't know what was next, but at least now, there was a chance to make things right with Jean.

And that, for the first time in days, felt like a step in the right direction.

*Jean*

The antiseptic scent of the hospital room was stifling, clinging to my senses like an unwelcome shadow. I blinked my heavy eyelids open, feeling like I'd been dragged from the depths of a troubling dream. The fluorescent lights above buzzed with relentless energy, stark and unforgiving. My head throbbed in sync with the beep of the monitor by my side.

I could make out fragmented conversations around me, the voices jumbled and overlapping. One was firm and authoritative, a police officer demanding consent for a toxicology test. Another was deeper, Frederick's voice asserting that I'd never drive drunk—he knew I was allergic to those cursed flowers.

A third voice cut in that belonged to Elvis. "Why don't you just leave her alone? The accident was my fault. I've already owned up to it. I should have never been texting while driving." The tension in the room was palpable, almost suffocating.

I managed to crack open an eyelid, only to be met with the sterile white walls of the hospital room and a TV monitor mounted high, its flickering light a harsh contrast against the stillness. An oxygen mask was strapped to my face, delivering an intermittent stream of air that felt both alien and comforting.

I fumbled with it, trying to pull it away, my throat burning with the effort.

"Who does Elvis text?" I rasped, the question escaping my lips with a ragged edge. My voice was barely more than a whisper, but it was enough to catch the attention of the room.

"Jean!" Frederick's voice was cut with an intensity that made my heart skip a beat. His strong, large hands grasped mine, his touch warm and grounding. He adjusted the oxygen mask back over my face with a tenderness that contrasted sharply with the chaotic energy in the room. His lips brushed my forehead in a soft kiss, and I felt a wave of relief wash over me.

Frederick's presence was a beacon of calm in the storm, and I could see the lanky police officer's frustration as he pressed the nurse call button on the wall. Elvis glared at the officer and crossed his arms over his chest, the sequined costume shimmering under the harsh fluorescent lights.

A nurse in blue scrubs entered, her gaze softening as she made eye contact with me. "We're awake, I see," she said, navigating around the men in the crowded room. "Let's check your vitals." She approached my bed, and I shifted but found one of my wrists shackled, the metal cuffs clinking against the glossy white bedrail. I tugged in disbelief.

The policeman stepped forward. "I need to inform you that

if you decline to consent to a toxicology draw to test for the presence of alcohol—"

"—She is not drunk," Frederick's voice cut through again, firm and resolute. His anger was palpable; his concern for me evident in every line of his face.

"No, she's not." A man in a white coat appeared behind Elvis, his salt-and-pepper mustache twitching as he assessed the situation. "It was a severe allergic response. With your consent, Ms. Price, I'll share the ER's tox report."

I pulled the oxygen mask away again. "Yes," I managed to croak.

The doctor glanced at his clipboard. "Diphenhydramine and epinephrine, which the ambulance crew administered on site. That's all."

"Now," Frederick demanded, turning to the police officer and gesturing toward the handcuffs. "If you don't mind."

The policeman reluctantly dug a key from his pocket and unlocked the cuffs, the metal clinking against the bedrail as he tucked them back into his belt. "I'll still need a statement."

"That can wait a bit, can't it?" Elvis chimed in. "Why don't we go grab a cup of coffee?" The officer shrugged, and both he and Elvis left the room.

I tugged at the mask again. "Can I take this off?"

The doctor stepped over to the beeping monitor and pressed

a button. "Yes, that's fine. I'm Dr. Roland." He settled onto a stool beside my bed and unwrapped his stethoscope, the cold metal making me flinch as he checked my vitals. "Good," he said after a moment. "Can you sit up for me?"

With a groan of discomfort, I eased myself up. My body protested, but the nurse helped steady me. Dr. Roland listened to my lungs, his stethoscope cold against my skin. "Deep breath. And again. Okay, you can lay back." He smiled at me beneath his mustache. "Do you know that you are severely allergic to flowers in the Asteraceae family?"

"Yes," I said, sheepishly. "I have been since I was a child."

"You were in close proximity to a large amount of them," he said, raising an eyebrow.

"David needed a different casket spray delivered to the funeral home and—" My breath caught in my chest. "Edgar's funeral! What time is it? Are the flowers ruined?" I struggled to move in my panic, and Frederick caught my hand.

"Jean, it's nearly four o'clock in the afternoon."

My heart twisted in my chest. I'd missed the funeral. It was over and done with hours ago. Tears began to stream down my face.

"Next time, Ms. Price, take only the recommended dose of Benadryl. Get some rest and avoid those flowers." Dr. Roland slid the stool against the wall. "We're going to monitor you for

190

just a bit longer," He said on his way out the door.

"Thank you," I said, my voice small. I scanned the room, searching for my belongings. "Is my purse here? My phone—"

Frederick stood and moved to a maroon upholstered chair in the corner. "Elvis brought it with him after the accident," he said, his voice steady. "I rode in the ambulance with you."

"Thanks," I said awkwardly as he handed me the purse. "For staying with me, I mean. I don't remember much after getting out of the car. How is that you were so close?"

"I was on my way to breakfast, and I saw you driving." He took my fingers in his, lifted them to his lips, and brushed a tender kiss over my knuckles. The touch sent a shiver through me, my heart racing with a sudden, sharp awareness. The monitor's beeping next to the bed increased, as if echoing my emotions. "You had me worried there for a while."

My face warmed with a deep blush, and I dug my phone out of my purse, my fingers trembling slightly. There were no missed calls or texts from David. My heart sank and the despair must have been evident on my face.

"Jean," Frederick said softly. He sat down on the edge of the bed next to me as I shoved my phone back in my purse. The tears were welling up in my eyes, and I refused to look at him.

He placed a gentle finger under my chin and moved my focus to him. The tears spilled over.

"David put you in harm's way deliberately."

I shook my head, biting my lip. "No, he wouldn't have. It had to have been Beth somehow."

The corner of Frederick's mouth twisted. "Whether it was him or Beth, he seems to be allowing her to play this cruel game with you."

My face and what little reserve I had left crumpled. He gathered me against his chest as I cried, overwrought. My sobs shook through me, muffled against Frederick's chest. The scent of his cologne, something woody and comforting, only made the pain sharper, reminding me of all the ways David had failed to offer that same comfort, that same protection. Why did I keep defending him in my mind? Every excuse I made for him chipped away at what I thought I knew, at the version of him I still hoped existed.

Frederick's arms tightened around me as if he could sense my thoughts spiraling. I pulled away slightly, wiping at my eyes with the back of my hand, trying to regain some dignity, though it felt far beyond my reach now.

"I thought—" my voice cracked, and I swallowed thickly, "I thought we were stronger than this. That after everything we'd been through at work for the last six years, and then it seemed like we were finally getting going. I thought we'd at least...talk." I looked down at my lap, my vision blurring with tears. "But he just—nothing! No apology. Nothing!"

"Jean," he said softly, "David's silence is his answer."

I flinched at the bluntness, but deep down I knew Frederick was right. David's silence had become deafening, each hour without a word from him confirming what I feared most. The weight of it settled into my bones, making my chest feel tight, like I couldn't draw a full breath.

"Maybe he's protecting me in his own way," I said, though even I wasn't convinced. The words tasted bitter.

Frederick exhaled sharply, releasing me and standing. He paced the room, his frustration palpable, but I couldn't meet his eyes. "And how well is that working out, Jean?" he asked, his voice low but tense. "You're unraveling because of him, and you're still making excuses. This is breaking you apart."

I pressed my palms into my thighs, trying to still the shaking. I didn't want to admit it. But the truth was staring me in the face. What did it say about me that I still wanted David, even after everything?

Frederick stopped pacing, coming back to sit next to me, his hand resting lightly on mine. His voice softened again, almost pleading. "Jean, you don't deserve this. You deserve better than someone who leaves you twisting in the wind, who allows others to hurt you. You know that, don't you?"

I closed my eyes, Frederick's words sinking in, but they

didn't give me the relief they should have. Instead, I felt hollow, like I was losing a part of myself by letting go of David, even if he was already gone.

"Where do I go from here?" I whispered, my voice so small I wasn't sure he even heard me. I wasn't asking about logistics. I was asking how I was supposed to rebuild everything that had crumbled over these past few days—my trust, my sense of security, my belief that David and I were on the same side.

Frederick squeezed my hand gently. "One step at a time, Jean. But the first step is letting go of what's hurting you."

I bit my lip, tasting the salt of my tears, and nodded. But inside, I wasn't sure I had the strength to take that step, to let go of David, Shep and Son, and everything that had tethered me to a life that now felt so far out of reach.

Someone cleared their throat. I glanced toward the door, where Elvis stood with a cup of coffee in each hand, steam curling up to meet his thick black sideburns. He looked slightly uncomfortable, glancing around the room.

"No, come in," I said, wiping my eyes on the back of my hand and gesturing him forward.

Elvis stepped in, handing a cup of coffee to Frederick.

"Thanks," he said.

Elvis looked at me. "I'm really sorry about rear-ending you. I shouldn't have been texting and driving. It's just...well, my girlfriend and I were having an argument, and she sent me all these messages, and—"

"I'm fine," I said, squeezing Frederick's hand and giving him a quick glance. "I know what those kinds of texts can do to a person."

"I have insurance. I've given all my info to Frederick here. You won't have to pay for anything. I'll even replace those flowers if you—"

"No," I said with a short laugh. "No more flowers."

"Okay, well, like I said, you've got my number. If you need anything at all, don't hesitate to call me."

"Thank you," I said. He apologized a few more times before he left, and I shook my head, a smile playing on my lips. "What are the odds?"

"I don't know," Frederick said with a laugh. "How many Elvis impersonators are there in the greater Elmburn area?"

My stomach suddenly growled, and we both laughed, as I sniffed away the last of my crying jag.

"Can I get you something to eat? If the nurse says it's okay, of course?"

I nodded, feeling both emotionally drained and physically exhausted. "Yeah, something light would be good. Hospital food can't be worse than the day I've had."

He smiled, his face softening, and stood up. "I'll head down to the cafeteria. I won't be long."

He stood from his seat on the side of the bed, his hand lingering on mine for a moment longer than necessary. His eyes held mine with an intensity that made my breath catch in my throat. He hesitated, as if weighing his next words carefully.

"Jean," he began, his voice low and measured, "I don't want you to think I'm pushing you, especially not now, but... I need you to know something."

I blinked, waiting for him to continue, unsure where this was going but feeling a knot tighten in my stomach.

He took a breath, running a hand through his hair as he paced a few steps away, then turned back to face me. "The real reason I came to Shep and Son for my publishing in the first place... it wasn't just about the company's reputation or the contracts they offered. It was you, Jean."

I frowned, confused. "Me?"

Frederick nodded. "When I was researching publishers, your track record stood out. You've made a name for yourself, more than you know. And when I started asking around, other publishers had noticed you too. They were impressed with your work. I was impressed."

I opened my mouth to speak, but nothing came out. The room felt suddenly smaller, like his words had filled the space between us with an invisible weight.

"And then, when I finally met you," he continued, stepping closer again, his voice soft but steady, "I realized that this wasn't just about a professional connection. Jean, there's something here—between us. Something worth exploring."

My pulse quickened, the implications of his words sinking in. My mind raced, trying to keep up with the shift in the conversation. I wasn't ready for this, not now. Not after everything with David.

Frederick sat down again, this time closer, his hand resting gently on my arm. "I know things are complicated right now. I know you're grieving the loss of what you had with David and Shep and Son. But I want to make you an offer. Come with me to Florida. Work with me. You can take some time for yourself first—God knows you deserve a vacation—but then, when you're ready, we can start fresh."

I stared at him, the words spinning in my head. Florida? With Frederick? My mind flooded with thoughts—what that would mean for my career, for my life, for...us.

"I don't want you to feel pressured," he added quickly, sensing my hesitation. "But I can give you what you need, Jean. The time, the space, whatever you want. I just... I think we owe it to ourselves to see what this could be—both professionally and personally."

His gaze was so open, so genuine, it was hard to look away. Part of me wanted to say yes, to leave all the mess behind and start over somewhere new, with someone who saw me, who valued me. But then there was that other part, the part that was still tangled up in the pain of David's betrayal, in the guilt of leaving behind six years at Shep and Son, the friendships, the memories.

I looked down at my hands, feeling the weight of the decision he was asking me to make. "Frederick," I started, my voice shaky, "I don't know if I can do that. It's tempting, but… I just got out of a relationship that was tangled up with business. And look where that got me."

He nodded, his expression softening but still hopeful. "I understand. I do. But this is different. I'm not David. I'm offering you something real, something where you get to set the terms. And we're both honest with each other at that the start that we're attracted to one another."

I bit my lip, considering his words. It wasn't that I didn't trust Frederick—I did, more than I wanted to admit—but I wasn't sure I trusted myself not to repeat the same mistakes. To lose myself in someone else's world, to let my professional life become inseparable from my personal one.

"I'm not asking for an answer right now," he said gently, as if sensing my inner turmoil. "Just think about it. Take the time you need. But you don't have to go through all of this alone."

He stood up, brushing his hand lightly across my shoulder as he did. "I'll get you something to eat. You need to regain your strength."

I nodded, still too overwhelmed to speak, and watched as he left the room. His offer hung in the air like a lifeline, and yet, all I could feel was the weight of what I'd be leaving behind if I took it.

David, Shep and Son, the life I'd built for six long years—how could I walk away from all of that? But how could I stay, when staying meant more of the same silence, more of the same heartbreak?

As the door clicked shut behind Frederick, I realized that, sooner or later, I would have to choose.

***

*David*

My apartment was quiet. It felt like a tomb, like the silence of the grave we'd set my father down in. I threw my jacket onto the back of the nearest chair and roughly tugged the knot of my tie loose, my mind still caught in the uncomfortable tug-of-war between grieving for my dad and all the mistakes I'd made to lose Jean.

My fingers tapped the edge of the dining table, restless and anxious as I checked the messages on my phone. I hadn't expected to get a call today from Donelson's agent insisting a call back no matter the hour when I received the message.

Even though it was late, I dialed his number, hyping myself up for the familiar dance of egos and negotiations. Jake Ross's voice was clipped, polite, but with an edge that hinted he was ready to play hardball.

"David, we need to talk."

"Sure. I was under the impression everything was signed, sealed, and delivered. That we were ready to move ahead."

"I'll be blunt, then. We're reconsidering the deal."

I stopped pacing. "Reconsidering? Jake, your team signed the contracts. What's there to reconsider?"

"The pitch, David. The whole concept. Donelson loved it, and frankly, so did I. It's why we came to Elmburn and bypassed The Big Five. But our legal team's been looking into things, and they've come to a conclusion: Jean was the brains behind that pitch. She's the only one who can deliver on it."

My grip tightened around the phone. So Jean had told Donelson or his team about my firing her. "I'm not sure what you heard, Jake, but—"

"The deal's off, Shep." Jake's words hit like a sucker punch. "We need Jean on board. Without her, we don't trust Shep and

Son can handle the execution. It's nothing personal, David, but she was the one who really sold it."

"I'm telling you, I can deliver."

"You think so," Jake said, voice almost pitying. "But we need more than confidence. Our lawyers are clear: without Jean, you're in breach, and we can back out clean."

"You're making a mistake," I snapped, but I could feel the edges of my bravado crumbling. I'd known Jean was good, but this—this was something else. "Everything's already in place. We have the strategy, the mockups, the—"

"All Jean's work. She's the creative genius here, David. You've got until tomorrow to figure it out. If she's not involved, Donelson's out."

The line went dead.

I tossed the phone onto the table, resisting the urge to slam my fist down after it. The worst part was that Jake wasn't wrong. Jean's vision had transformed my shoddy, run-of-the-mill proposal into something game-changing, something that had Donelson seeing dollar signs and prestige. Without her, this deal was as dead as my father.

I grabbed my keys and bolted out the door. If Jean was the missing piece to this, then I had no choice but to bring her back in, even if it meant swallowing every ounce of pride I had left.

Jean lived in a small, quaint house in the suburbs that

matched her practical yet creative nature—warm, unassuming, and easy to overlook if you didn't know what you were looking for. I rang the bell and waited. I knocked, then pounded when no one answered. I pressed my ear to the door, listening for any sound of movement inside. Nothing. The house was dark.

"Damn it, Jean," I muttered, fishing my phone out of my pocket again. I scrolled through my contacts, thumb hovering over her name. This wasn't an apology that I wanted to make over the phone. I had to find out where she was so that I could do this in person. I scrolled to George Price, her brother.

He picked up on the second ring. "David."

"George, where's Jean? I need to talk to her. It's urgent."

There was a pause, the kind that sends a shiver up your spine because you know it's not going to be good news. "She's in the hospital."

My heart lurched. "What the hell happened?"

"She was in a car accident, David." His voice was strained, and I could hear underlying anger simmering. "Jean picked up the new casket spray like you asked this morning—even though she was allergic as hell to it. She had a reaction while driving and got rear ended. She had an ambulance ride to the hospital."

The shock hit me like a tidal wave. "I never asked her to get any flowers, George. I wouldn't do that. I know she's allergic."

George pushed on, words laced with frustration. "She's

been trying to help you in every way possible for years, even when it means hurting herself. But I swear, today's world has a million ways to communicate, and yet, somehow, you two fail every time."

"That's not—"

"Save it," George cut in. "You've had every opportunity to see Jean for who she really is—the best damn thing that's ever happened to you, whether you deserve it or not. She's loved you since the day she met you, even if you've been too busy to notice."

I couldn't find the words to argue, to deflect, to do anything but absorb the truth he'd thrown at me. George was right; I'd missed every signal Jean had ever sent, and now she was paying the price.

"Which hospital?" I finally asked.

He told me and gave me the room number, and I hung up, my head spinning. On my way out, George's comment about communication—about all the miscommunications—stuck with me like a thorn. It echoed in my mind, gnawing at something I couldn't quite put my finger on until I opened my contacts again, scrolling down to the card I'd used more times than I could count over the years.

I hit the info button in the top corner. Jean's number wasn't on the screen. It was *Beth's.*

203

I stared at it, the reality of what I was seeing sinking in like a slow poison. Beth had switched the numbers. My stomach twisted at the thought of how many conversations I thought I'd had with Jean, only to realize it had been Beth manipulating every word, every request. And Jean—she'd probably been getting the same twisted messages on her end through Beth.

I scrolled through messages, seeing the subtle changes, the questions I'd sent thinking they were directed at Jean, and Beth's answers that had sent everything spiraling. No wonder she'd picked up a casket spray full of flowers that sent her into a reaction. I never asked her to, but I would bet the publishing house itself that Beth had.

Jean and I had finally connected at the skating rink after I sent the email message that had taken Beth out of the equation. And then our time in person, together, at my father's house, when we'd made love after she'd walked me through all those sorting and remembering tasks—God, how had I taken that for granted? How had that not been foremost in my mind through that damn suit incident?

I didn't know whether to punch something or throw my phone into the street and run it over. Beth had orchestrated this disaster from the shadows, playing us both for fools. And here I was, stuck with the fallout.

The drive to the hospital was a blur of frustration and guilt.

Every red light felt like it was conspiring against me, every second ticking by a reminder of how badly I'd screwed this up. By the time I pulled into the parking lot, my mind was racing with how I'd even begin to fix this—if it could be fixed at all.

I parked and sat there for a moment, gripping the steering wheel, staring at the sterile, unwelcoming façade of the hospital. Jean was inside, hurt because of me—or, more accurately, because of the chaos I had allowed Beth to scheme between us. And now, as much as I wanted to burst in there and make everything right, I couldn't even begin to figure out how to apologize for this colossal mess.

As I stepped out of the car, my phone buzzed again—a message from Jake Ross: *If Jean's out, we're out.* He'd given me an ultimatum: bring Jean or lose everything I'd been working for. Dammit. Even if the Donelson deal stood, I wasn't confident Shep and Son would survive without Jean and my dad. I wasn't anywhere near enough. And hiring someone to replace her?—there was no replacement. I was such a fool.

I shoved the phone back into my pocket and stared at the hospital's entrance. The sliding doors opened and closed automatically, people moving in and out, even at this late hour, lost in their own worlds of worry and relief. I took a deep breath and stepped forward, feeling the weight of every decision I'd made dragging behind me like chains. I had no idea what I was going to say to Jean, or if she'd even want to hear it.

All I knew was that somewhere in the mess of contracts, miscommunications, and broken trust, I had to find a way to make things right. The future of Shep and Son depended on it. But more than that, Jean deserved better—better than what I'd given her, and better than the lies we'd both been fed.

I pushed through the hospital doors, uncertainty tightening around me. A rush of hot, sterile air slapped me in the face. The buzz of fluorescent lights and the sharp scent of antiseptic filled my senses, adding to the chaos in my head. My chest felt tight, like I'd been punched in the gut and was still struggling to catch my breath. My dad was gone, his funeral barely behind me, but that pain was nothing compared to what I felt when I heard Jean was in an accident. And it was my fault—at least, it felt that way.

I pushed past the front desk, ignoring the receptionist's attempts to catch my attention. I didn't have time for small talk or protocol; I just needed to see her, to explain, to fix whatever mess I'd made.

After a few wrong turns and a curt exchange with a nurse who seemed determined to slow me down, I finally found Jean's room. But just as I was about to push the door open, it swung wide, and I nearly collided with *Frederick Donelson!* The sight of him hit me like ice water down my spine.

"What the hell are you doing here?" I blurted, my voice sharper than I intended.

Donelson looked every bit the billionaire: impeccably dressed, with the kind of confidence that comes from having the world at your fingertips. But his presence here, in Jean's hospital room, felt wrong. Out of place.

"Jean needed help," Donelson said, his voice calm, infuriatingly composed.

I couldn't believe what I was hearing. Jean had called him? This wasn't just business. I could see it in the way he said her name, with a softness that made my blood boil.

"And you just came running, huh?" I snapped, trying to keep my voice low even as it threatened to break. "Do you have any idea—"

"I know exactly who you are," Donelson interrupted, his expression shifting from cool to cutting in an instant. "David Shep, head of Shep and Son Publishing. Let's see...A company coasting on your father's name, nearly run into the ground. Your list of accomplishments is short, but your list of failures? Now that's impressive."

His words stung, and I hated how accurate they were. But this wasn't about me or my failing company; this was about Jean, and Donelson was treating her like she was his.

"The only reason we even entertained the idea of working

with Shep and Son was because of Jean Price," Donelson continued, his voice cold and confident. "She's got the talent, the vision. You were riding her coattails, and you didn't even realize it."

"That's not true," I said, though even I'd already come to the conclusion myself, but I wasn't about to admit to this cocky jerk.

"Isn't it? She was the one who pitched us, the one who sold us on this entire project. And yet, you've been playing these childish games with her. The suit stunt, firing her, and now this nonsense with the flowers."

I froze, my mind racing. How did he know all this? And more importantly, why did he care so much?

"You think this is some sort of game?" Donelson continued. "Jean deserves better than whatever circus you're dragging her through."

"You don't know anything about what's going on between us," I shot back, my voice rising despite myself. "I never asked Jean to pick up those flowers. I didn't do any of this. It's all been a twisted setup by someone who hates us both."

"Beth?" Donelson arched an eyebrow, clearly unimpressed. "Your ex-fiancée and Jean's step-sister?"

"Yes," I said firmly, but the conviction in my voice felt thin, even to me.

Donelson shook his head. "Do you even hear yourself? You've let a woman as incredible as Jean be pulled into your massive drama, and you don't even see it. It's pathetic. She deserves better than to be a pawn in whatever sick scheme you and Beth are playing at."

"You don't get to talk about her like that," I snapped, my fists clenching. "Jean is not some damsel in distress for you to rescue."

Donelson smirked, and it was the kind of expression that made my blood boil. "I'm not rescuing her. I'm respecting her— something you clearly don't know how to do."

I wanted to argue, to shout, to tell him that he had no idea what Jean and I had been through, but his words hit too close to home. And the way he talked about her, like she was someone he genuinely cared for—it twisted something in my chest. Jealousy, raw and unfiltered, surged through me.

"I'm going to see her," I said, stepping toward the door.

"Be my guest," Donelson said, his tone mocking. "But don't be surprised if she doesn't want anything to do with you."

I pushed past him, opened the door, and stepped into the room. Jean was shrugging into her coat as a nurse held out a clipboard with what I guessed was discharge paperwork. Her face was pale, and her eyes lacked the fire and light I was so used to. She turned her focus to the door after I opened it. For a moment, she looked at me, and I thought—hoped—that maybe she'd be glad to see me. But then her expression hardened.

"What are you doing here?" she said, her voice weak but laced with irritation.

"I—I heard what happened," I stammered, trying to keep my voice steady. "Jean, I'm so sorry. I didn't—"

"—Go away," she interrupted, her tone flat, dismissive. "I don't want to see you. Not now, not ever."

Her words hit me like a slap. Her anger reminded me of my own that I'd let loose on Beth at the funeral home. I opened my mouth to argue, to explain, but the look on her face stopped me cold. She wasn't just angry; she was done.

Donelson stepped in behind me, his presence looming. "You heard her," he said quietly. "It's time for you to leave."

I glanced back at Jean, desperate for some sign that this wasn't the end. But she'd turned her face away from me, finishing up with the nurse. Donelson was right; she didn't want me here.

As Donelson ushered me out, he caught the attention of a security guard, who started making his way toward us. My frustration boiled over.

"Jean, please!" I called out as the guard grabbed my arm. "Check your phone. Look at my contact card. You'll see—it's all been Beth! She's been messing with us. We didn't even have a chance."

But Jean didn't respond. The door swung shut behind me, and the guard tightened his grip, leading me toward the exit.

I wrenched free, spinning around to face Donelson. "This isn't over," I snarled, my anger flaring hot. "You think you can just swoop in and take everything? You don't know anything about me, about us."

Donelson's expression remained infuriatingly calm. "You're right, David. I don't know much about you. But I do know that Jean deserves better than this."

I couldn't hold back anymore. Everything—my dad's death, Beth's schemes, my mistakes, Jean's accident, Donelson's smug superiority—boiled over. I swung at him, my fist aimed right for that self-satisfied look on his face. But Donelson dodged, quick as lightning, and returned the punch with a precision that sent me sprawling to the ground.

Pain exploded through my jaw, and I tasted blood. I lay there, staring up at the hospital's bright lights, feeling lower than I ever had in my life. A second security guard rushed over, pulling me up and dragging me toward the exit, but I couldn't stop looking back at Donelson.

He stood there, composed, barely winded, like I was just another inconvenience he had to deal with. I hated him in that moment, not just because he'd gotten the better of me, but because he'd stepped into the role I'd failed to fill—the person who was there for Jean when she needed someone most.

As I was shoved out of the hospital doors and into the cold night, I felt like I'd hit rock bottom. Everything I'd worked for, everything I thought I had, was slipping away. Jean, my company, my damn dignity—it was all crumbling.

But Donelson's parting words echoed in my ears, a challenge I couldn't ignore:

"Figure out who you really want to be, David," he'd said. "Because right now, you're not even close to being the man Jean deserves."

And as security shoved me through the doors and into the winter cold, bruised, humiliated, and alone, I knew he was right. I had to fix this. I just didn't know how.

# Chapter Seven

*Jean*

The gentle hum of the jet engines was a constant, soothing backdrop as I settled into the plush leather seat of Frederick Donelson's private plane. Everything about it screamed luxury: the cream-colored interior, the glossy wood paneling, the soft lights that cast a warm, inviting glow. It was a world far removed from the chaos of my life back in Elmburn, and exactly what I needed—a perfect, temporary escape.

I glanced out the window, watching the clouds drift by like lazy cotton balls. Below us, the world looked small and distant, and for the first time in weeks, so did my problems. It was hard to believe that less than twelve hours ago, I was in a hospital bed, surrounded by the wreckage of what felt like my life. But now, miles above the ground and heading toward a sunny Florida vacation that Frederick had insisted upon, everything felt lighter. Even manageable.

Frederick sat across from me, casually flipping through a file chock full of documents Jake had given him. But he was clearly more interested in me than in any paperwork. His presence was magnetic, impossible to ignore. He was the kind of man who filled any room, or in this case, any aircraft cabin, with an air of quiet authority and charm. His brown eyes, sharp and attentive, flicked up to meet mine.

"Comfortable?" he asked, a smile tugging at his lips.

"Yes, thank you," I replied, forcing a smile of my own. "This is…incredible."

He chuckled softly. "It's just a plane, Jean. But I'm glad you're enjoying it."

I nodded, but my mind was far from settled. I'd checked David's contact card on my phone after he'd caused the scene at the hospital. It was true—Beth had swapped his number with hers, manipulating us both in ways I hadn't imagined possible. She'd orchestrated every miscommunication, every hurtful moment, all to drive a wedge between us. But David's outburst at the funeral home was still his own doing, and the memory of him firing me without a second thought—believing I'd betrayed him—still stung.

Frederick's voice pulled me back to the present. "You've been through a lot," he said, his tone gentle, almost protective.

"And I can see how all this mess with David and Beth has taken its toll on you."

I sighed, running a hand through my hair, which still felt limp and stringy after the hospital. "It's been a nightmare," I admitted. "I can't believe how quickly everything fell apart."

Frederick leaned forward, his expression serious. "I want you to think about something, Jean. You're talented, driven, and frankly, wasted in your current situation. You deserve better than being caught up in someone else's drama."

His words felt like balm on a wound. I had worked so hard to build my career and establish myself in the publishing world, and to be reduced to a pawn in Beth's manipulative game, yet again, was a humiliating slap in the face. I felt like that pathetic, awkward girl sprawled in the middle school quad again.

But there was more to it than that—David's lack of trust, his willingness to believe the worst of me without question, cut the deepest.

"I'm not sure what to do next," I said honestly, my gaze falling to the glass of sparkling water in front of me. "I thought I knew where my life was going. Now I'm not so sure."

Frederick placed the file he'd been holding on the table between us and leaned back, studying me with those penetrating eyes. "I've been thinking about something for a while," he said slowly, deliberately. "The publishing industry needs a shake-up, and I've got the resources to make that happen. But I need someone with vision, someone who knows the ropes. I need you, Jean."

I blinked, stunned. "What are you saying?"

"I'm saying I want to start my own publishing company," Frederick said, his tone confident and warm. "And I want you to head it. You'll have complete creative control, access to the best resources, and the freedom to build something truly remarkable."

I stared at him, speechless. It was more than just publishing his works, which would have set me up for life. It was the kind of offer that most people only dreamed of—an open invitation to create something from the ground up, backed by one of the most powerful and kindest men I'd ever met.

Frederick's voice softened, taking on a more personal note. "I've seen your work, Jean. I've seen the way you handle yourself in a room full of people trying to outsmart you. You're brilliant. And I believe in you."

I felt my cheeks flush, a mixture of pride and disbelief warming my chest. No one had ever spoken to me like that, least of all in my professional life. With David, I'd always felt like I had to fight to prove myself, to be seen as more than just a coworker.

"I don't know what to say," I managed, my voice catching

in my throat. "This is…unbelievable, Frederick. But it's a lot to consider."

He smiled, leaning forward slightly. "Of course it is. I'm not asking for a decision right now. But I want you to know that the offer is real, and it's not going anywhere. Take all the time you need."

I nodded, overwhelmed by the magnitude of his proposal. The rest of the flight crew bustled quietly around us, offering drinks and snacks, their presence professional and unobtrusive. It was clear that everyone on this jet respected Frederick deeply. The captain had even come out to greet him personally when we boarded.

As the plane continued its smooth journey southward, I found myself relaxing into the seat, feeling a weight lift off my shoulders that I hadn't realized I'd been carrying. It wasn't just the luxury or the escape from Elmburn—it was the realization that I had options, that I was no longer trapped by David's doubts or Beth's schemes.

But as freeing as that was, the question still lingered: Could I really walk away from everything? From David?

Frederick's eyes were on me, watching my reaction carefully. "I know this is a lot to process, Jean. And I know you've got history with David, complicated as it is. But do you still feel you owe him your loyalty after everything he's put you through?"

I swallowed hard, his words hitting closer to home than I wanted to admit. "I know," I said, my voice barely above a whisper. "But it's not just about loyalty. It's..." A silence hung between us, though not awkwardly.

"It's love, isn't it?" Frederick finished for me, not unkindly. He let the words hang between us, not rushing me to confirm or deny. "I understand, Jean. I've been in love. And I've been let down by the people I trusted most. It's not easy to walk away."

I met his gaze, searching his eyes for judgement but finding none. "How do you do it?" I asked. "How do you keep going when the people who were supposed to be there for you turn out to be...something else?"

Frederick's smile was tinged with a sadness that made him suddenly seem his older age and more human. "You learn to rely on yourself," he said quietly. "And you surround yourself with the right people. People who see you, who value you. You've already proven you're strong, Jean. You just need to let go of those who drag you down."

The sincerity in his voice made my throat tighten. Frederick wasn't just offering me a job; he was offering me a way out. A chance to start fresh, away from the mess David and Beth had pulled me into. But what did that mean for my feelings? Could I really just walk away from the life I'd built in Elmburn, even if it was in ruins?

Frederick's voice pulled me back from my thoughts. "I don't expect you to forget him," he said softly, almost as if he could read my mind. "But you don't have to let him define you, either. You're better than that, Jean. And you deserve to be happy."

I looked at him, really looked at him, and saw not just a billionaire with a penchant for control but a man who'd lived through his own losses and somehow come out the other side— and yet here he was, still fighting, still building.

"Why are you being so nice to me?" I asked, my voice cracking. "You barely know me."

Frederick shrugged, his smile soft and genuine. "Maybe I just see something in you that reminds me of someone I used to know. Someone who deserved better."

His words settled over me, heavy but comforting. I finally felt seen—not as part of a business, not as someone's employee, but as myself.

As the jet began its descent toward the sun-drenched coast of Florida, I knew that whatever decision I made, it would be for me and no one else. I had a lot to think about, and time was on my side. But I knew one thing for sure: I couldn't go back to the way things were. Not after everything that had happened. Frederick was right. I deserved better.

*\*\*\**

*David*

Sitting alone at Shep and Son, the silence felt like a weight on my chest. The framed pictures on the wall, the worn leather chair that had been my father's, the pile of paperwork that never seemed to shrink—it all felt like it was mocking me. This was supposed to be the family legacy, the dream my father had built, but right now it felt like a prison. I stared at the whiskey glass in front of me, the amber liquid catching the late afternoon light, and wondered for the hundredth time how everything had gone so wrong.

Jean was gone. She was the heart and soul of this place, the one person who could talk me down when I was too caught up in my own head. And now, thanks to my own stupidity, she'd taken a private jet with Frederick Donelson, flying off to a life I could never give her. She was gone, and so was the deal that was supposed to save this company from going under. The irony wasn't lost on me—losing Jean had cost me everything.

It wasn't just the Donelson deal. It was the way everyone in the office looked at me now, like I was the idiot who'd let the best thing that ever happened to Shep and Son slip through his fingers. And they were right.

I ran a hand through my hair, feeling the tension thrumming

in my veins. I knew, deep down, Jean would never have pulled that stunt with my dad's suit. She loved my father. She'd written his obituary with a reverence and understanding that even I couldn't capture. She saw the best in him, just like she'd seen the best in me, once. But I hadn't listened. I hadn't trusted her. Instead, I'd let Beth's manipulations poison my mind, and now I was paying the price.

Beth. I'd cut her out of my life completely—blocked her number, deleted every trace of her from my contacts, my social media, everything. I couldn't believe I'd let her get this close, let her twist my reality into something so unrecognizable. But even that wasn't enough to fix things. Beth was just the symptom of a larger problem. The real issue was me. I was the one who'd doubted Jean. I was the one who'd let my own fears and insecurities drive her away.

I took a long drink of the whiskey, letting the burn slide down my throat, but it didn't bring the clarity I was hoping for. All I felt was a crushing sense of loss. The employees at Shep and Son missed Jean, and they weren't shy about letting me know it. Morale was at an all-time low, and I couldn't blame them. Without Jean's steady hand, her calming influence, everything felt off-kilter. The staff was frustrated, disorganized, and I could see the resentment simmering just below the surface. They all knew what I'd done, and they didn't respect me for it.

I leaned back in my father's chair, staring up at the ceiling, the old cracks and faded paint telling their own story of neglect. What was I going to do? How was I going to stabilize this company without her? Could I even handle the employees as a boss, without Jean there to smooth things over, to make everything seem less… hopeless?

The truth was, I didn't know. Every decision felt wrong. Every attempt to move forward felt like slogging through quicksand. And worse, I realized I'd been thinking about Jean all wrong. I'd been treating her absence as just another problem to solve, another missing piece of the puzzle for Shep and Son. I was only thinking about what she could do for the business, how much we needed her skills, her talent, her organizational magic. But I hadn't thought about Jean as Jean.

I hadn't thought about her as the woman who laughed at my stupid jokes, who knew how to calm me down when I was one second away from losing it. I hadn't thought about her as the woman who saw the good in me, even when I couldn't see it myself. Jean wasn't just some asset to be leveraged. She was a beautiful, kind, fiercely intelligent woman who, for reasons I'd never quite understood, had chosen to be a part of my life. And I'd thrown that away.

I thought back to the look on her face at the hospital when

she told me to leave. I'd tried to explain, to get her to understand that Beth had played us both, that none of it was real. But Jean's reaction was her own—wounded, angry, and so deeply disappointed in me. She'd seen what I couldn't, or maybe wouldn't: that I'd failed her. Not just as her boss, but as the man she once cared about. The man she'd trusted.

I set the glass down on my desk, the ice clinking as I leaned forward, resting my head in my hands. I'd never felt more lost. The truth was, Jean had loved me once, and I'd thrown it all away because I couldn't see past my own insecurities. She was everything I'd ever wanted—smart, compassionate, driven. She was everything I wasn't, and that scared the hell out of me. It was easier to believe she'd betrayed me than to face the fact that I was the one who'd let her down.

I picked up my phone, scrolling through the missed calls, the unanswered texts I'd sent her since that day. Each one felt like a desperate attempt to patch a hole that was already too wide to fix. I wanted to tell her I was sorry, that I'd been blind, that I didn't know how to do any of this without her. It wasn't enough. It was never going to be enough.

The office door opened, and I looked up to see Andrew, one of our editors, hovering uncertainly in the doorway. "Hey, David," he said, his tone hesitant. "Do you have a minute?"

I nodded, gesturing for him to come in. "Yeah, what's up?"

Andrew shifted nervously, holding a stack of manuscripts. "We're behind on a lot of projects," he said. "I've been trying to keep things on track, but without Jean..." He trailed off, the implication hanging in the air.

"I know," I said, running a hand over my face. "I'm sorry, Andrew. I'm trying to get things back on track."

He nodded, but I could see the doubt in his eyes. "I know you are. But Jean... she held everything together, you know? She made this place feel...I don't know, like a team. Like we were all in this together."

I swallowed hard, the weight of his words sinking in. Jean had been the glue that held Shep and Son together, and now that she was gone, the cracks were starting to show. "I'll figure it out," I said, though I wasn't sure I believed it myself. "Just... bear with me."

Andrew nodded. "You know, I, uh, feel it's only right to tell you up front since you'll probably be getting some phone calls. I've applied to a few other publishing houses. I just don't think I have a place here anymore."

I nodded in response, not trusting myself to speak, and he left, closing the door softly behind him. I stared at the manuscripts he'd left on my desk, but the words blurred together, meaningless in the face of everything else.

I reached for the phone again, my thumb hovering over her

name in my contacts. She'd moved on. She was with Donelson now, and who could blame her? He was offering her a chance at something bigger, something better. Something I couldn't give her, no matter how much I wanted to.

I tossed the phone aside, frustration boiling over. I couldn't keep going like this, stuck in an endless loop of regret and doubt. I had to figure out a way forward, for the company, for myself. But every time I tried to make a plan, to see a path out of this mess, all I could think about was her. Jean, with her calm smile and her sharp wit, her unshakable belief in me, even when I didn't deserve it.

And that was the hardest part—knowing that she'd believed in me when I didn't believe in myself. Knowing that I'd thrown away the best thing that had ever happened to me.

Without her, I didn't know who I was anymore.

*** 

*Beth*

I leaned against the styling chair, twisting a strand of hair around my finger as Susan Danvers went on and on about her latest drama at the country club. She was in every other week to touch up her highlights, but she treated my chair like a confessional booth. Today was no different. I nodded along, pretending to care about the tennis court politics, but my mind was somewhere else entirely.

It had been a few weeks since everything had gone down with David, Jean, and the funeral home mess, and I was starting to feel... well, restless. Sure, I'd stirred the pot in a way that only I could, but it hadn't given me the satisfaction I thought it would. If anything, I felt oddly empty. Like I'd eaten the cake but it was made of air.

"Did you hear about your ex?" Susan's voice suddenly cut through my thoughts, her tone dropping into that conspiratorial whisper that all these society ladies seemed to think made them sound more important. I straightened up a little, my interest piqued.

"What about David?" I asked, trying to sound casual as I brushed out a section of her hair. David's name on her lips didn't surprise me; his family had been a fixture in this town for decades, and everyone loved a good story about the Sheps, especially when it wasn't flattering.

Susan glanced around the salon, as if she were worried someone else might overhear. "Oh, honey, it's a mess. You remember Cindy? Cindy's husband works over at the bank that handles Shep and Son's accounts. Well, she was at lunch with Becca, you know, Becca who's married to that guy who owns the car dealership, and she says that David's just losing it. The business is falling apart without Jean Price. I mean, I'm not surprised, are you? Jean was always the brains of the operation."

I froze, holding the brush still in Susan's hair as her words hit me. David struggling without Jean? That was exactly what I'd wanted. I'd wanted him to see that he was nothing without me. Without us. But it wasn't feeling as sweet as I thought it would.

"Really?" I said, trying to keep my voice light. "What do you mean by 'falling apart?'"

Susan leaned closer, her eyes lighting up as she reveled in the gossip. "Oh, he's losing clients left and right. No one's happy with how things are being run. And apparently, he's been trying to get Jean to come back, calling her, texting her, but she's completely ignoring him. Good for her, I say. He fired her, after all! Imagine firing the one person keeping your whole business afloat. That's David Shep for you. I can't believe the two of you lasted as long as you did!"

I turned away for a moment, grabbing a bottle of hairspray, but really I was trying to hide the sudden twist in my gut. This wasn't supposed to be about Jean winning. This was supposed to be about me. About me getting the life I wanted. I had been the one playing the long game, working behind the scenes, making sure Jean was out of the way. And now? Now she was on some pedestal again, just like always.

"That's crazy," I said, trying to keep the annoyance out of my voice. "But honestly, it's kind of predictable. David's never been great with managing anything, especially not people." It was the kind of remark that usually got Susan to nod along in agreement, but she was too caught up in her own version of events to notice my discomfort.

"And get this," Susan continued, lowering her voice to a whisper. "Jean's not even here anymore. She's in Florida! With Frederick Donelson. You know, the billionaire?"

"What?" My heart skipped a beat, and I nearly dropped the curling iron. I quickly regained my composure, setting it back down carefully, but my mind was spinning. Jean with Frederick Donelson? I'd heard the deal had gone south for David, but the idea of Jean involved with someone like that? The kind of man who could buy and sell everything David owned with pocket change? It was...well, it was infuriating.

Susan continued, oblivious to the shock I was trying to hide. "Oh yeah, I guess they've gotten pretty close. He's practically whisked her away to paradise. Can you imagine? Some people just land on their feet no matter what."

I plastered on my best fake smile and tried to laugh, but it came out sounding hollow, even to my own ears. "Jean always did have a way of bouncing back." And wasn't that the truth? Every time I thought she was down, she found a way to crawl back up again, like some unkillable weed that just wouldn't stay pulled.

But as Susan kept talking about her latest Pilates class and her upcoming trip to Cabo, I could barely focus. I went through the motions of styling her hair, nodding and smiling at the right moments, but my mind was a million miles away. Jean was in Florida with a billionaire. David was drowning without her. And me? I was here, listening to someone else's gossip, living the same day on repeat, like I was stuck in a loop that I couldn't break free from.

I finished up with Susan, watching her prattle on about this or that, and suddenly it all felt so…small. Trivial. As she left the salon, her hair perfectly coiffed, I felt this strange heaviness settle over me. I couldn't tell if it was regret, or anger, or something else entirely, but it lingered.

I sat down in the empty styling chair, staring at my reflection in the mirror. I looked the same as I always did—put together, polished, like I had everything under control. But inside, I felt raw and exposed. I'd spent so much time trying to control everyone else's lives, bending them to fit into the version I wanted, and now I was left with nothing but the pieces.

I thought about David, his weaknesses, his insecurities. Sure, I'd been furious when he hadn't crawled back to me, but had I really wanted to marry him? To spend my life with someone who could barely keep it together, who always seemed to need someone else to prop him up?

I'd never been the kind of person who wanted to compromise, to settle down and play the dutiful partner. I wanted freedom. I wanted to live life on my own terms, to do what I wanted, when I wanted, without answering to anyone. That was what made me happy—no strings, no obligations, just me and whatever I felt like doing in the moment. I thought about all the schemes I'd pulled, the manipulations, the lies. What had they really gotten me? A front-row seat to someone else's drama, and a whole lot of emptiness.

I leaned back in the chair, crossing my arms as the realization started to sink in. I'd been chasing the wrong things. David, Jean, all of it—it was just noise. I'd thought I wanted revenge, that I wanted to come out on top, but the truth was, Jean was going to be fine no matter what I did. She was too kind, too optimistic. She'd find a way to make everything work out for her. People like her always did.

What about me? I'd always prided myself on being the one pulling the strings, but now I wasn't so sure. What if, instead of constantly trying to tear other people down, I just...stopped? What if I let go of all the grudges, the petty rivalries, the need to prove that I was better than everyone else? I didn't want to be tied down, not to David, not to anyone. And maybe, just maybe, it was time I started living like it.

I picked up my phone, scrolling through my contacts until I found David's name. He'd blocked my number after the hospital fiasco, and I hesitated now, my finger hovering over the screen. I could use my shop's landline. Part of me wanted to call him, apologize, and explain why I'd done what I'd done. But another part of me—the part that was finally starting to see clearly—knew it wouldn't change anything. David was struggling, but it wasn't my job to fix him. It never had been.

I put the phone down, letting out a breath I didn't even realize I'd been holding. Maybe what goes around does come around, but I was done waiting for karma to even the score. I didn't need to keep up this endless cycle of games and grudges. It was time to figure out what I wanted, without dragging everyone else into my mess.

As I looked at my reflection, I saw something I hadn't seen in a long time: the possibility of something different, something better. Not for David, not for Jean, but for me.

***

*Jean*

The night air in Florida was warm, perfumed with the salt of the sea and the sweet scent of gardenias that spilled from perfectly manicured hedges surrounding the terrace. The band played softly in the background, each note of the violin lingering in the humid air like a whispered promise. I could still feel the soft vibrations of the music against my skin, the gentle thrum of the bass and the warm buzz of conversation just beyond the dance floor.

Frederick's hand rested at the small of my back, guiding me through the steps of a slow tango with effortless confidence. He moved with the kind of grace that only came from years of experience and the poise of someone who had spent a lifetime navigating ballrooms and boardrooms alike. His touch was firm yet gentle, commanding yet tender—an unexpected and intoxicating combination that made it easy to forget about the rest of the world.

I let my body melt into his, allowing myself to be led. My emerald green dress swirled around my legs with every pivot, its silk fabric catching the candlelight and shimmering like liquid jade. Frederick looked at me with those intense, mocha brown eyes, dressed in a suit that was impeccably tailored, probably worth more than I'd made in a month at Shep and Son. But he wore it as effortlessly as a second skin, the dark fabric cutting a striking figure against his broad shoulders and lean frame.

This was my life now—or at least, it had been for the past month. Days filled with languid mornings on the sun-warmed sands of a private beach, afternoons lost in the steamy worlds of romance novels that had absolutely nothing to do with work, and evenings like this one, dripping with decadence and delicious, stolen moments.

Frederick had wined and dined me, whisked me off to the finest restaurants, and indulged my every whim. He had orchestrated this escape with a deft hand, making sure I had the space I needed to unwind. There were no expectations, no pressure, just the quiet reassurance of his company. And despite my initial reservations, I had come to enjoy Frederick's presence more than I cared to admit.

The music swelled, and he spun me in a slow turn, our movements synchronized in perfect rhythm. The world seemed to shrink to just the two of us, surrounded by the flickering glow of candles and the soft strains of music. I couldn't remember the last time I'd felt so carefree, so completely untethered from the demands of reality. Frederick had handled everything: the reservations, the arrangements, even the simplest of decisions. All I had to do was exist, and for the first couple of weeks, that had been enough. Lately though, the dreaded B word had started to creep into my day. I was starting to get *bored*.

As we danced, I glanced up at him, taking in the lines of his face. He was handsome, undeniably so, but it was his quiet confidence that had drawn me in. The way he looked at me— as if there was no one else in the room, as if I was the only thing worth his attention—made my pulse quicken. And when he spoke, his voice was always a low, comforting rumble, a sound that wrapped around me like a warm embrace.

"You've been quiet," he said, his voice gentle as he pulled me closer. "What's on your mind?"

I hesitated, the truth stuck somewhere between my heart and my throat. I wanted to tell him that I was grateful, that I hadn't felt this relaxed, this free, in a long time. But the words didn't seem enough, and instead, I smiled, letting the music speak for me.

"It's just perfect," I finally said. "Everything is so beautiful."

His gaze softened, and for a moment, the air between us felt charged with something unspoken. "I'm glad," he replied, his hand brushing lightly against my back as we glided across the floor. "I've enjoyed this time with you, Jean. More than you know."

I nodded, unable to articulate the knot of emotions tangled up inside me. Frederick's offer—the chance to start a new publishing house, to build something entirely my own—had been on my mind since the day he first mentioned it. But more than that, it was his quiet companionship that had gotten under my skin. The way he seemed to understand what I needed without my having to say it.

The tango slowed, and he dipped me gently, his breath warm against my cheek as he pulled me back up. I laughed softly, feeling the thrill of the movement, the delicious closeness of him.

"You're good at this," I teased, trying to keep the mood light.

He smiled, his eyes crinkling at the corners. "I've had practice."

The music built again, and we moved as one, our bodies swaying together in perfect harmony. I was so caught up in the moment, in the way his hand fit against mine, in the soft, lingering scent of his cologne, that the word slipped out before I could catch it.

"David," I whispered, my voice barely audible over the music. "This is..."

Frederick stilled, his steps faltering ever so slightly. I felt the change immediately, a sudden coolness that snaked between us. He didn't pull away, but his grip tightened just enough for me to notice. The realization hit me like a punch to the gut, and I could feel the blood drain from my face.

"I'm so sorry," I stammered, mortified.

Frederick straightened, his expression inscrutable. He didn't look angry, but there was a sadness in his eyes that hadn't been there before. He let out a slow breath, and when he spoke, his voice was calm, almost resigned.

"Jean," he said quietly, his gaze searching mine. "Are you ever going to be able to forget him?"

I swallowed hard, unsure of how to respond. Frederick's question hung in the air between us, heavy and unanswerable. I looked down, avoiding his eyes, my thoughts a tangled mess of memories and regrets.

"I don't know," I admitted finally, my voice trembling. "It's not that simple."

Frederick led me to the edge of the dance floor, away from the other couples, and we stepped out onto the wrap-around patio, approaching the railing overlooking the water. The moonlight glinted off the waves, casting a silver sheen over the dark expanse of the ocean. He turned to face me, his expression gentle but unwavering.

"Tell me about him," he said, leaning against the railing, his posture relaxed despite the tension in the air. "Tell me about what makes him stick in your mind."

I hesitated, feeling exposed under his scrutiny. But there was something in Frederick's eyes—something that told me he genuinely wanted to understand, not just judge. And so, I let the walls I'd built around my heart start to crumble.

"He was so…different. Smart, ambitious, a little reckless. But he had this quiet balm about him, this way of toning me down. He helped me see that even without all my spreadsheets and calendars and lists, I could still achieve what I needed to. I admired him so much, and I think I fell for him almost instantly."

Frederick listened quietly, his gaze never leaving mine. I could see the questions forming in his eyes, but he didn't interrupt. I continued, the memories spilling out in a rush.

"But I never told him," I admitted. "I watched him from a distance, pretended I was okay just being his coworker at first, then his friend—eventually his confidant. I watched as Beth...nabbed him up. I thought I could handle it, but..."

I trailed off, the words sticking in my throat. I looked out at the water, my heart aching at the weight of all the things left unsaid. Frederick's hand found mine, and I felt a warmth spread through me at his touch, a silent reassurance that I wasn't alone in this.

"Why didn't you ever tell him how you felt?" Frederick asked gently.

I shook my head, feeling foolish. "I was scared," I confessed. "Scared of losing him, of ruining what we had. And maybe I thought if he really wanted me, he'd figure it out. But...he didn't. Or maybe he just didn't feel the same way."

Frederick's thumb brushed over my knuckles, his touch steadying me. "That sounds like a lot of weight to carry on your own."

"It was," I whispered. "And when things went wrong—when Beth came into the picture—I felt like I was losing him. But the truth is, I never really had him to begin with. Obviously, or we could have made it through all the miscommunications with Beth."

Frederick's expression softened, and he squeezed my hand gently. "Jean, maybe you've been holding onto an idea of him, of what you thought he could be. But the man you loved, the man you've built up in your mind...he might not be real. He might only exist in your expectations."

I blinked, trying to process his words. It was something I had never considered, not fully. I had always seen David as this perfect, unattainable figure—a man who, in my mind, could do no wrong. But the reality was messier, more complicated.

Frederick's voice cut through my thoughts, low and earnest. "There's a man right in front of you who wants to be here, who wants to know you—really know you. Not some perfect version of you, but the real thing. And he's ready to love you if you'll let him."

My breath hitched, and I looked up at him, really looked at him. The kindness in his eyes, the patience in his smile—it was all there, plain as day. Frederick had been nothing but honest with me, never hiding his interest, never making me feel like I was second best. And yet, I had been so wrapped up in my own pain, in my past with David, that I hadn't allowed myself to fully see what was right in front of me.

"I don't want to rush you," Frederick continued, his voice gentle but firm. "But I need to know, Jean. Can you let him go? Can you make room for something real, something right here and now?"

I didn't have an answer—not yet. But as I stood there, feeling the warmth of Frederick's hand in mine, the rhythm of the ocean waves lapping against the shore, I knew that the choice was mine to make. For the first time, I felt the faint stirrings of hope, the possibility of something new, something wholly my own.

"I don't know if I can forget him," I said honestly, my voice barely above a whisper. "But I want to try."

Frederick's smile was soft, his eyes gleaming with a quiet tenderness that always seemed to speak louder than words. As he nodded, he pulled me gently into his embrace, his arms wrapping around me in a way that felt both secure and delicate, as though he was afraid to break the fragile intimacy of the moment. The world around us seemed to slow, the ocean breeze carrying the distant hum of waves crashing onto the shore. It was as if the beach itself held its breath, waiting to see what would happen next, though in that instant, the only thing that mattered was us.

We stood there together, the warmth of his body grounding me as the evening breeze playfully tugged at my hair. The music from the dancefloor drifted into the background, blending with the natural rhythm of the ocean, but it no longer seemed relevant. This moment belonged to us. I could feel the steady rise and fall of Frederick's chest as he breathed, the subtle connection between us deepening with every heartbeat. It felt as though the universe had conspired to bring us to this exact point in time, to give us this rare chance to be completely in sync with one another.

I allowed myself to lean into the moment, letting go of the worries that usually tugged at the back of my mind. There was no past or future, no uncertainty or doubt—just the present, and the quiet intensity of his presence beside me. His hand gently traced the line of my back, and I let my head rest against his shoulder, feeling the comforting weight of him. The quiet promise in his touch reassured me in ways words never could, a reminder that we didn't need to speak to understand what was unfolding between us.

The salty air brushed against our skin as Frederick slowly lowered his lips to mine, his kiss soft and unhurried, like the waves caressing the shore. It was a kiss that spoke of patience and understanding, a tender exchange filled with the kind of care that made me believe in something bigger, something lasting. The ocean whispered behind us, as though it too had secrets to share, but in that kiss, all that mattered was him, and the quiet, unspoken promise of what we could become—if I could just forget.

# Chapter Eight

*David*

I woke up on the couch to the dull, throbbing headache that had become as familiar to me as the bottle of whiskey on the coffee table. The sun was already high, stabbing through the blinds in angry slashes of light that cut across the floor, illuminating the mess I'd made of myself and my apartment. Empty bottles, takeout containers, and a pile of unopened mail cluttered the living room, all of it a testament to the fact that I hadn't bothered to go into work for...how many days now?

Shep and Son was crashing and burning, and I was doing absolutely nothing to stop it.

I reached for the half-empty bottle of whiskey, my hand shaking just enough to spill a few drops onto my already stained shirt. I took a swig, letting the burn scorch my throat, numbing everything inside. The alcohol didn't help like it used to. It wasn't enough to drown out the memories of Jean or the echo of my father's disapproving voice. But it was better than nothing.

I was halfway through my drink when I heard the sharp, insistent buzz as someone leaned on the bell downstairs. I ignored it at first, hoping whoever it was would just go away, but it continued, until it was clear that whoever was on the other side had no intention of leaving.

"David, open up!" Beth's voice cut through the apartment's intercom, and I cursed under my breath. She was the last person I wanted to see.

I dragged myself toward the panel, the room spinning slightly with every step. Before I made it, I heard the ding of the elevator, and then suddenly, there she was—Beth, in designer dress and heels, her expression a mix of frustration and determination. She pushed past me without waiting for an invitation, her nose wrinkling at the stench of stale booze and unwashed dishes.

"God, David," she said, looking around the apartment with thinly veiled disgust. "This is how you've been living?"

"How'd you get in here?"

"Beau, your super."

I shuffled back to the couch and slumped down, taking another swig from the bottle. Beth followed, her heels clicking against the hardwood floor, her eyes never leaving me.

"You didn't show up to work. Again," she said, crossing her arms over her chest. "I talked to some of the employees at Shep and Son. They say you've been letting everything go to hell."

"Why do you care?" I muttered, not bothering to look at her. "Last I checked, it's my company to run into the ground."

Beth let out a frustrated sigh, running a hand through her meticulously styled hair. "David, you need to wake up. You need to shape up. This—" she gestured to the mess around us, "—this is not you."

I laughed bitterly, the sound harsh and humorless. "You don't know a damn thing about me."

She frowned, her brow furrowing as she stared at me. "Why? Why are you letting everything fall apart like this? Is it about your father? Or is it Jean?"

I clenched my jaw, the mention of Jean's name sending a fresh wave of anger and regret crashing over me. I threw back another swallow from the bottle, feeling the familiar burn. "It's not about my father," I said quietly, my voice laced with bitterness.

Beth paused, her eyes flickering with something I couldn't quite place—pity, maybe, or guilt. For a moment, I thought she might actually leave me alone, but then she surprised me by sitting down on the edge of the coffee table, facing me directly.

"I'm sorry," she said, her voice softer now but with no hesitation. "I never really wanted you, David. You have to know that. I just...I didn't want Jean to have you."

I looked up at her, the words sinking in slowly, like poison. "What the hell are you talking about?"

Beth's gaze faltered, and she glanced down at her perfectly manicured hands. "I've hated Jean ever since our parents got married. She always had this way of just...standing there, taking everything I dished out at her. I thought it was weakness, like she was too spineless to fight back. But now..." She trailed off, biting her lip.

I watched her, the sudden vulnerability in her expression so foreign that I almost didn't recognize her.

"But now?" I prompted, my voice low, laced with anger and exhaustion.

Beth looked up, meeting my eyes. "Now I realize it wasn't weakness at all. It was strength. Jean never let me get to her. She never stooped to my level, no matter how hard I tried to provoke her. And I hated her for it. I hated her for being better than me."

I scoffed, leaning back into the couch. "I don't give a damn about your apologies or whatever sudden enlightenment you've had. You ruined everything. All I want is Jean back, and that's never going to happen. She's gone. On some private beach in Florida with a billionaire who's giving her everything she ever wanted. And I'm stuck here, in this godforsaken apartment that I'll probably default on, with nothing."

Beth's face tightened, her expression hardening. For a moment, I thought she might lash out, but then she let out a long, measured breath. "You're right. I did ruin everything. But I'm going to fix it."

I laughed again, a short, bitter bark. "You? Fix it? Don't make me laugh."

She stood up, smoothing down the front of her dress. "I mean it, David. I'm going to get you a front-row seat to plead your case to Jean. But you'd better damn well be ready to show up and fight for her."

I stared at her, disbelieving. "And why the hell would you do that?"

Beth hesitated, and for a second, I saw a flicker of something genuine in her eyes. Regret, maybe, or the last vestiges of whatever conscience she had left. "Because I owe it to her. And to you. And because, believe it or not, I'm tired of all this bullshit."

She turned to leave, her heels clicking against the floor with every step. When she reached the door, she stopped, looking back at me one last time. "I'm picking you up at six. Shower, shave, get rid of that whiskey stench, and put on something that doesn't look like you've been sleeping in it for a week. If you really want her back, you'd better be ready to show her."

I watched as she left, the door clicking shut behind her. For a long moment, I just sat there, staring at the space she'd occupied, the apartment suddenly feeling even emptier than before.

I looked at the whiskey bottle in my hand, the last few swallows of amber liquid sloshing at the bottom. I raised it to my lips, intending to drain it dry and forget every word Beth had said, but something stopped me. A flicker of hope, a spark of defiance, a whisper of something I hadn't felt in what seemed like forever.

Maybe it was the thought of seeing Jean again. Maybe it was the idea that I still had a chance to explain, to make her see that I was still here, still fighting, even if it was only by the thinnest of threads. Or maybe it was just that, for the first time in weeks, someone was giving me a way out of this hellhole I'd made for myself.

I set the bottle down, the clink of glass on wood reverberating through the quiet room. I got up, moving slowly, every part of my body protesting, heavy with the weight of everything I'd lost and everything I still stood to lose.

The bathroom was a mess, but I didn't care. I turned on the

shower, the water blasting ice cold at first before warming to something bearable. I stripped out of my rumpled clothes, tossing them to the floor, and stepped under the spray. The water hit my skin, washing away the grime, the stench of whiskey, and, for a moment, the suffocating fog that had settled over me.

I braced my hands against the tiles, the water streaming down my back as I let my head hang forward. I closed my eyes, feeling the sting of regret and the sharp edge of desperation. Jean's face flashed in my mind, her smile, the way she used to look at me when she thought I wasn't paying attention. The way she'd always been there, a quiet, steady presence in my life, even when I didn't deserve it.

I stayed in the shower longer than I should have, letting the water pound against me, willing it to wash away the past, to give me the strength to stand up and fight. For her. For us.

By the time I stepped out, the mirror was fogged over, obscuring my reflection. I wiped it clean with my hand, staring at the man looking back at me. He was a stranger—tired, beaten, worn down by his own choices. But there was still a flicker of something in his eyes, something that hadn't been there in a long time.

*Hope.*

I shaved, trying to make myself look halfway presentable. I

pulled on a clean shirt, the fabric stiff from lack of wear, and a pair of pants. I combed my hair, the simple act of grooming feeling strangely foreign, like I was trying on a new skin.

By the time six o'clock rolled around, I was ready. Or as ready as I could be, waiting for Beth to show up. I didn't know what she had planned, didn't know yet what I'd say to Jean if I got the chance, but I knew one thing for sure: I couldn't keep going like this. I couldn't keep losing myself to the bottom of a bottle, letting everything I cared about slip through my fingers.

The buzzer sounded, and I grabbed my keys, took one last look around, and headed for the door.

Whatever happened next, I was going to fight. For Jean. For us. And maybe, just maybe, for the man I used to be before I let everything go to hell.

Beth was right about one thing—I had to shape up. And tonight, I was going to start.

\*\*\*

The hum of the jumbo jet's engines droned in the background as I sat next to Beth, watching her scribble in her notebook like a woman on a mission. The thick cloud cover intensified the darkness of the night outside. No stars, no moon visible in any of the states we soared over so far. I pulled down the window shade and shifted in my seat, trying to get comfortable, but something about Beth's intensity kept me on edge.

She looked up from her notes and gave me a determined look. "David," she said, voice steady but with a playful edge. "Do you know as much about Jean as she knows about you?"

I raised an eyebrow, not sure where this was going. "I'd like to think so," I replied, cautious but admittedly curious. What was she getting at?

Beth grinned, clearly scheming something. "I'm planning something big. Something really showy, borderline ridiculous even, but in a way that'll show Jean you actually see her. Not just like anyone else does—but really see her. We're going to send three gifts ahead to Florida. Something based on the stupid poems she likes. The ones by that woman that always wrote about death."

I furrowed my brow. "You mean Emily Dickinson?" I knew she was Jean's favorite poet.

"Yes. She used to go on and on about her when we were in high school. Such a bore. Now, which poem is her favorite?"

I didn't even have to think about it. I knew. Jean had a framed copy of it on the wall in her office. "'There's a Certain Slant of Light.'"

"Okay, pretend you know her better than anyone. All those little things no one else sees. But first, let's start with the poem. What does it mean to her? What's the connection?"

I leaned back in my seat, letting my mind drift to all those conversations with Jean about Emily Dickinson's poem. I knew it by heart now, the way the winter light was described, that cold, sharp beauty that felt so far away yet so personal.

"The poem is about light," I began, feeling my way through it. "It's something elusive, almost painful but beautiful at the same time. Jean loves the way it describes that slant of light in the winter, the way it changes everything—makes it all sharper, more intense, heavier. It's a metaphor for wanting something you can never quite have. And when that something leaves for good, it leaves the emptiness of death."

"Mmhmm." Beth gave me a look that stabbed the center of my guilt.

I glared at her. "Where are you going with this?"

"Right. So we need the first gift to embody that—the feeling the poem gives her."

I took a deep breath, frustrated.

"Don't overthink it. Close your eyes."

"This is stupid—"

"—Just do it."

I sighed. "Fine."

"Now, clear your mind." She was quiet for a moment, then, "If I say *Jean* and *light*, what's the first thing you think of?"

"Stained glass." I opened my eyes, surprised.

"Why?" Beth sat, pen at the ready to take notes.

"We were working on a how-to book about different art forms, and stained glass was one of the chapters," I started to explain. I remembered the day Jean and I met that stained glass artist like it was yesterday. Jean had been relentless in tracking down the best of the best, and somehow, she found this small studio tucked away in the arts district, owned by a woman named Lydia.

The studio was a hidden gem—sunlight streaming through half-finished pieces hanging from the ceiling, throwing colors across the room. I remember being in awe of the way the light played through the glass, each shard catching the sun in a different way, bending it into something more beautiful. Lydia was an older woman, with silver hair and these gentle but strong hands that had clearly worked glass for years. She walked us through the delicate process like it was second nature, explaining how every piece told a story through light. Jean was taking notes furiously, as usual, while I stood there mesmerized, absorbing every detail of the craft.

Jean and Lydia clicked immediately, talking about the precision and patience required to create each piece. Jean had a way of drawing people out, asking the kinds of questions that made Lydia's eyes light up with pride in her work. We spent the entire afternoon there, Jean sketching ideas for the book, and me listening to the two of them talk about art, life, and everything in between. When we left, I couldn't stop thinking about how stained glass was like poetry in color—fragile, elusive, but breathtaking when the light hit just right.

It was funny—thinking about that now, with Beth planning the elaborate gift for Jean, it all circled back. That day in Lydia's studio, surrounded by shards of glass and fragments of light, felt like the seed of this idea. Maybe we'd been building up to this moment all along, without even realizing it.

"The light changes it into something distant yet present. Jean said the stained glass captured it in this haunting, beautiful way. It's fragile but solid, kind of like how the light passes through in the poem—leaving a mark but never staying."

Beth's eyes lit up. "That's perfect. A stained glass sculpture or window piece. Something delicate but full of color, so it catches the light just right. But we have to have it delivered in some kind of snappy way."

I leaned forward and put my elbows on my knees. I thought of something but knew Beth would scoff at it. "No, it's stupid."

"We're open to anything and everything at the moment. It needs to be something she would never expect. Something that is going to get into her head that she won't forget."

"Well, she wouldn't forget it, but I have no idea how we'd manage it."

"Leave the logistics to me."

I shrugged. "Okay. The poem talks about the weight of cathedral tunes. So—"

"—a choir," we said together.

"Perfect," Beth said, unfazed. She scribbled down a few more notes. "Consider the first gift done. Now, onto the second."

We continued brainstorming, and I couldn't believe what we ended up with—or how Beth was going to pull it all off. When I questioned her again, her expression softened. "David, these gifts are going to knock her off her feet. More than that, though—they're from someone who knows her inside and out. You've been there for her all this time, maybe not with the same attachment she's had to you, but if this doesn't get her to listen, I don't know what will."

I looked away, staring at the closed window. "I hope you're right."

Beth reached over and gave my arm a reassuring squeeze. "Trust me."

I let out a breath. Trusting her was either the worst or the best idea of my life. Her confidence was contagious, and I felt a flicker of hope. Maybe this would begin show Jean how much I truly cared. Not just with words, but with actions that spoke to her soul.

Beth was already flipping through her notes, fine-tuning the details of each gift, while I opened the window shade, staring out at the darkness, wondering if this could be the moment that changed everything. As the plane hummed along its path to Florida, the possibilities felt endless.

*** 

*Jean*

Frederick and I were just stepping out of his mansion, ready for a quiet evening at the movies, when the unexpected happened. The evening was mild, the sky a soft shade of violet with a few stars peeking through, but just as we reached the driveway, I heard the sound of footsteps coming from the garden path. A group of five people emerged from around the corner, dressed in flowing gold and white church robes, moving in perfect harmony like they were part of some divine procession. My heart skipped a beat at the sight of them, my curiosity instantly piqued.

Before I could say anything, they began to sing. It wasn't a typical sing-o-gram like you'd expect at a birthday party or as a joke gift—it was a Latin church hymn, rich and resonant, each note filling the evening air with reverence. Their voices blended together, a chorus that felt at once ancient and alive, as though it belonged to some grand cathedral rather than Frederick's

255

manicured front lawn. I felt the vibration of their harmonies deep in my chest, the kind of music that makes you stop in your tracks and listen.

I glanced at Frederick, expecting to see some hint that this was a surprise he had arranged, but his face showed only confusion. He furrowed his brow slightly, his lips parting as if to ask me what was happening, but the music kept us both silent.

As the hymn swelled, one of the singers stepped forward, holding something large and wrapped delicately in thick brown paper. I could see the edges of it beneath the wrapping—something glassy and delicate, refracting the fading sunlight. When they reached us, the lead singer, a man with a voice as deep as a bell, presented the gift to me with a bow, still singing. My hands, almost moving of their own accord, reached out to take it.

The glass was cold and heavy in my hands, and the weight of it sent a thrill down my spine. I didn't want to interrupt their song, but my fingers itched to tear the wrapping away. As the last note of their hymn faded into the evening, they turned silently and walked back the way they had come, leaving me standing in the driveway with this beautiful, mysterious gift and Frederick, still looking as bewildered as I felt.

I wasted no time. Slowly, carefully, I began unwrapping the

layers of paper, and when the last piece fell away, I gasped. It was a stained glass window—an intricate, detailed scene of a gnarled tree, its branches twisting and curling in an almost tortured fashion. The glass shimmered in the fading light, deep greens and silvers giving the tree an ethereal, otherworldly quality. It was about three feet tall and two feet wide. The craftsmanship was exquisite, each piece of glass carefully chosen to create a haunting, almost melancholic beauty.

I ran my fingers lightly over the surface, careful not to press too hard on the delicate glass. There was no note, no indication of who had sent it, but something about the image struck me. Frederick was staring at it too, still silent, as though he were trying to figure out what it meant.

"It's exquisite," he finally said, though his voice carried a note of suspicion.

"It is," I murmured, still transfixed by the tree's twisting branches. And then, like a light flickering on, I realized where I had seen this imagery before. The gnarled tree, its haunting beauty—it was *exactly* what I'd always associated with Emily Dickinson's poem "There's a Certain Slant of Light." The connection hit me like a wave. There was only one person who knew how much that poem meant to me. David.

I looked up at Frederick, unsure whether to say anything about my realization. His brow was still furrowed, but now there was a hint of something else there—curiosity mixed with the faintest twinge of jealousy. I smiled, trying to keep things light. "It must be from David," I said quietly, though I wasn't entirely sure I wanted to explain why.

Frederick looked at me sharply, a flicker of something dark passing through his eyes. "David? Why would he send something like this? And with that choir?"

I shrugged, pretending to brush it off. "He knows I love Emily Dickinson's work, and there's a poem that...Well, it doesn't matter."

Frederick didn't say anything more, but I could sense his mood shift slightly. Still, he let it go, and, after I quickly ran the beautiful piece of stained glass to my room, we headed to the car for our movie—though my mind stayed with the gift.

The next morning, we were having breakfast out on the patio, the sun already beginning to warm the air, and the scent of fresh coffee and orange trees filled the space. Frederick had set out a beautiful spread—fruit, croissants, and eggs—and I was just starting to relax when one of his assistants approached with a large, beautifully painted box.

"For Miss Jean," the assistant said, setting it down in front of me. The box was striking, covered in a winter scene so realistic it looked like the air around it should have turned cold. Snow dusted bare trees and frost-covered the ground in tiny, delicate brushstrokes.

I hesitated before opening it, and Frederick watched with a wary look, his coffee cup paused halfway to his mouth. The second I lifted the lid, I froze. Inside, nestled in layers of crisp white paper, was a lemon meringue pie, but not just any pie. It was shaped like a coffin, anthropoidal in shape, the whipped meringue cut into crisp lines, with the bright yellow lemon curd peeking out from beneath. The meringue and inside of the box were dusted with some kind of edible gold flakes.

I stared at it, my heart pounding. I didn't need any further proof—this was another gift from David, and once again, it was tied directly to Dickinson's poem—the last two stanzas this time—clear as day to me and told through the guise of my favorite dessert.

I glanced up to find Frederick leaning over, his gaze flicking between me and the pie. He was watching me closely, and I could see the tension growing in his jaw. "Jean...what is that supposed to be?"

I smiled, trying to downplay the significance. "It's a lemon meringue pie," I said lightly, lifting it from the box. "David knows it's my favorite. He's just...tying it to the poem again, that's all. It's a bit of a stretch, but, you know him—he's always creative."

Frederick didn't smile. His eyes narrowed as he set his

coffee cup down, clearly trying to keep his jealousy in check. "He's going through an awful lot of trouble, don't you think?"

I shrugged again, playing it off.

But inside, I knew the gifts had hit me deeper than I was letting on. There was something about the thoughtfulness of them, the way David had chosen each one so carefully, that was making it hard for me to ignore how much he knew me—how much he still cared. I wasn't sure how I felt about that, but I couldn't deny the impact it was having.

Later that afternoon, we were getting ready to leave for a yacht party. Frederick was finishing up a call inside while I waited on the front steps when another delivery arrived. This time, the package was more straightforward—just a large plain brown cardboard box. I opened it without much thought, expecting something small, but as soon as I lifted the lid, I gasped.

Inside was a bouquet—not of flowers, but of books. Each cover was adorned with a delicate ribbon, and each had a flower in its title. *The Name of the Rose, The Scarlet Pimpernel, The Black Tulip* and a dozen others. It was a reader's dream bouquet, and it was breathtaking.

I ran my fingers over the spines of the books, my heart racing. There was no doubt about it now. David was sending me these gifts as more than just thoughtful gestures—they were declarations. Each one was a reflection of how well he knew me, how much attention he had paid over the years. It wasn't just about the poem. It was about us, and what had been left unsaid between us.

Frederick came outside just as I was closing the box, and I could feel his eyes on me as I tried to keep my expression neutral. "Another gift from David?" he asked, his voice tight.

I nodded, but before I could say anything, he made a low sound of frustration. "I don't like this," he muttered. "I don't like the way he knows you so well. It's like he's trying to prove something."

I closed the box and stood, turning to face him. "Frederick, it's just some gifts. David and I have known each other for a long time. It's not a competition."

But I could see it in his eyes—he felt threatened. He wanted to know me as well as David did, and I could understand that. I reached for his hand, giving him a reassuring smile. "I'm with you now," I said softly, hoping to ease his worries.

He nodded, but the doubt lingered. "I just want to know you on that same level," he said, his voice quiet but earnest.

I leaned in and kissed his cheek. "You will," I promised, though deep down, a part of me was already wondering what David was trying to say with these gifts—what message he was trying to send. And maybe more importantly, why a large part of me was listening.

***

*Beth*

I leaned back in the cab, my mind buzzing with the details of the plan I'd just put into motion. The driver navigated through the winding streets of Miami Beach, weaving between palm trees and high-end sports cars as the sun began to dip below the horizon. I watched the sky turn a molten gold, the kind of sunset you'd expect on a postcard—bright, beautiful, perfect. But all I could think about was the upcoming night and the high-stakes game we were about to play.

Crashing Frederick Donelson's exclusive party on his yacht wasn't exactly my idea of a good time. In fact, it was probably one of the most reckless stunts I'd ever pulled, but at this point, I was willing to do anything to get David in front of Jean. Even if that meant sneaking onto a billionaire's floating palace as a plus-one of a plus-one, just to get within spitting distance of the woman he couldn't stop pining for.

I adjusted my dress, a sleek black number that clung to me in all the right places. It wasn't the usual power suit I wore when I needed to get things done, but tonight called for something different. Something more convincing. The friend-of-a-friend I'd sweet-talked into getting us on board had given me a rundown of the guest list—celebrities, socialites, the kind of people who wouldn't even look at you if your net worth didn't have at least eight zeros. But I wasn't here to mingle or make connections. I was here for David. And for Jean too, though I still had a more challenging time swallowing that.

The cab pulled up to the hotel, and I stepped out, tipping the driver with a fifty-dollar bill I barely even looked at. I'd engaged him for the whole evening. Money was the least of my worries right now. I walked through the lobby, ignoring the glamorous tourists milling about, and headed for the elevator and our adjoining rooms. My heels clicked against the marble floor, echoing my rapid heartbeat. David better be ready. I'd just risked everything to make this happen, and I wasn't going to let him screw it up.

I opened the door of my room, the cool air of the room hitting me as I stepped inside. David was sitting on the edge of the bed, looking every bit like a man who'd just had the life drained out of him. He'd cleaned up since our conversation earlier in his apartment, and I had to admit he looked halfway decent in the crisp white shirt and tailored pants I'd picked out for him. But there was still that haunted look in his eyes, the one that told me he was barely holding it together.

"Everything's set," I said, closing the door behind me. "We're crashing Donelson's party tonight. I managed to get us on board as guests of...well, a friend of a friend. The orchestration isn't important. All you have to do is follow my lead and be prepared to talk to Jean."

David looked up, a mix of anxiety and hope flickering in his blue eyes. "You sure this is going to work?"

I shrugged, tossing my purse onto the chair by the window. "It's the best shot you've got. Donelson's security is tight, but he's the type who likes to show off. As long as we blend in and act like we belong, no one will ask questions. Just...don't do anything stupid. Or at least anything stupider than I will be doing."

He nodded, rubbing his hands together as if trying to warm himself up for what was coming. I watched him for a moment, noting the way his shoulders sagged, the uncertainty etched into every line of his face. It was strange seeing him like this—vulnerable, almost lost. David had been so put together, the kind of guy who walked into a room and owned it. But now, he was just a man desperately clinging to whatever hope was left.

"You're going to see her again," I said, softer this time. "And when you do, you need to make it count. Don't waste this chance."

He glanced at me, his expression shifting between gratitude and something else, something raw and painful. "Why are you doing this, Beth? You hate me. You hate her."

I crossed my arms, leaning against the dresser. "I don't hate either of you. Not anymore, anyway. I was petty. I was angry. Jean has always been the one for you, hasn't she? The stronger one. And I couldn't stand it. I spent years trying to make her miserable because it was easier than admitting that I was the one who was miserable."

He didn't say anything, but I could tell he was listening. Really listening. And maybe we were finally starting to understand each other, after all the fighting, scheming, and sabotaging.

"Look," I continued, feeling the weight of my own admission settle between us, "I've been a terrible step-sister to her. And a terrible girlfriend and fiancé to you. But Jean deserves better than to be stuck in some endless cycle of our crap. So do you. So, tonight, just go out there and tell her what she means to you. Be honest. It's the least you can do."

David's eyes flickered with something like hope, fragile and tentative. "Do you think she'll even listen?"

I met his gaze, feeling a rare pang of empathy that I hadn't allowed myself in years. "I think Jean's always listened. You just have to make her believe you're worth hearing."

David sat there, absorbing my words, and for the first time in a long time, I saw a spark of determination flare up in him. He wasn't quite the man he used to be, but he wasn't entirely gone, either. And that was something.

***

*Jean*

We stepped aboard Frederick's yacht, greeted by waitstaff dressed in black and white uniforms, carrying trays of champagne and cocktails. The ship was an overwhelming display of wealth and opulence, with every inch gleaming under the soft lights strung overhead. I felt a knot of unease twist in my stomach, and it wasn't just the champagne. Frederick had pulled out all the stops for tonight's party, his usual crowd of wealthy, self-assured guests mingling and laughing like they were on top of the world.

I was lingering near the edge of the deck, the ocean breeze cool against my bare shoulders, when I saw her. *Beth*. She was moving through the crowd with an ease that surprised me, blending in as if she belonged, though I knew she'd never been part of Frederick's circle. For a moment, I thought I was imagining her, but there she was, her dark hair perfectly styled, her eyes scanning the deck until they landed on me.

When she saw me, her face shifted, and she plastered on an expression of surprise that I might've once believed. She made her way over, her heels clicking on the polished deck, and I could see the slight tension in her movements. Something was off.

"Jean?" she said, her voice tinged with feigned delight. "I didn't expect to see you here."

"Beth," I said cautiously, my guard instantly up. "What are you doing here?"

She smiled, but it didn't quite reach her eyes. "I got an invite through a friend of a friend. I had no idea you'd be here. What a coincidence, huh?"

Frederick joined us, his presence immediate and commanding as always. He gave Beth a cool once-over, his expression calculating. He didn't know her, and I could tell he wasn't impressed by her sudden appearance. I'd seen that look before—Frederick was already sizing her up as a threat.

"You must be Jean's step-sister," he said, his tone flat, a clear sign that he was already suspicious. "I don't believe we've met."

Beth extended her hand with a polished smile. "Beth Oakley. I've heard so many great things about you."

Frederick didn't take her hand, keeping his expression neutral. "I wish I could say the same."

Beth dropped her hand smoothly, unfazed, and turned her attention back to me. "Jean, I'm glad I ran into you. There's something I've been meaning to say…and it's been a long time coming." She glanced at Frederick, then back at me. "Can we talk? Just the two of us?"

Frederick's eyes narrowed. He was protective of me, almost possessive, and he didn't like the idea of Beth having me alone. He was too savvy not to sense that something was wrong, but he also didn't know Beth like I did. He didn't know how she could worm her way into any situation.

"I'm not sure that's a good idea," he said, crossing his arms.

Beth flashed him a disarming smile. "I promise it won't take long. I just need a few minutes to clear the air. You understand, don't you?"

I glanced at Frederick, then back at Beth. There was something raw in her eyes that I hadn't seen in years, a vulnerability that I hadn't thought she was capable of anymore. Against my better judgment, I nodded. "It's fine, Frederick. We'll just be a minute."

He didn't look happy, but he stepped back, keeping a watchful eye on us as we moved away from the crowd, toward a quieter part of the deck. We walked in silence, the tension between us heavy and palpable. The sounds of the party faded behind us, replaced by the gentle lapping of the waves against the hull.

When we were finally alone, Beth stopped and turned to face me, her expression suddenly serious. "Jean, I want to apologize. For everything."

I folded my arms, unsure of where this was going. "Beth, I don't—"

"—No, please," she interrupted, her voice breaking slightly. "Let me say this. I've spent years being angry, and most of it was at you. But you didn't deserve that. You never did. I was the one who was jealous and bitter, and I took it out on you. I made your life hell because it was easier than dealing with my own issues."

I stared at her, taken aback by the sincerity in her words. Beth had never been one to apologize, not without an ulterior motive, but this felt different. There was a desperation in her voice that I hadn't heard before, and it made me hesitate.

"Beth, we've both made mistakes," I said carefully. "But you didn't have to—"

"—I did, Jean," she cut in, her voice trembling. "I needed to control something because I felt like I had no control over anything else in my life. But I see now how much damage I've done, not just to you, but to myself. I'm sorry. Truly."

The sincerity in her eyes caught me off guard. For the first time, I felt the walls between us crack just a little. She seemed so raw, so exposed.

"I appreciate that," I said softly, my voice barely audible over the ocean's whispers. "It means a lot, hearing you say that."

Beth smiled genuinely this time, and we fell into a moment of quiet, walking slowly toward the railing. It felt like the end of something and the beginning of something else—something uncertain, but hopeful.

"And I have to apologize one more time," she said quietly. "I promise this will be the last trick."

Before I could react, her hands shot out, shoving me hard. I stumbled backward, my body pitching over the railing as I tried to grab onto something, anything, to stop my fall. But it was too late. The cold shock of the salt water enveloped me, and I went under, the world above disappearing in an instant.

I fought my way to the surface, gasping for breath, the sound of the party muffled by the water in my ears. I looked up and saw Frederick on the deck, his eyes wide with horror after he sprinted toward the railing. He was going to jump in after me—I could see it in his face.

But Beth grabbed his arm, holding him back. "Don't," she snapped, her voice sharp with command. "Look."

Frederick stopped, confusion and fury warring on his face as he watched a small motor boat approach. It had been idling just thirty yards off, and now it was racing toward me. David was at the helm, his face stricken with worry as he reached down to pull me out of the water.

I was too stunned to fight, too shocked to do anything but

let him drag me into the boat, my wet clothes clinging to my skin. The engine roared, and before I could even catch my breath, we were speeding away from the yacht, the lights of the party growing smaller and smaller behind us.

On the deck, Frederick was shouting something, but I couldn't make out the words. Beth's figure was a shadowy silhouette against the glow of the yacht's lights, her face turned toward Frederick as she spoke to him. I couldn't hear what she was saying, but I could imagine. This was all part of some plan—her plan. And now I was right in the middle of it—*again*.

In the boat, David wrapped a towel around me followed by a life jacket, his eyes filled with a mix of relief and regret. "I'm sorry, Jean," he said, his voice barely audible over the rush of the wind, pounding of waves, and thrum of the engine. "I'm so sorry."

Drenched and shaking, I glared at him, my mind struggling to process everything that had just happened. All I could think was that I'd been played—by Beth, by David, by everyone. But there was something else too, a flicker of recognition that maybe this was the conversation I'd been avoiding for too long. And now there was no escape.

\*\*\*

*Beth*

Frederick paced, his fists clenched, every bit the powerful man used to being in control. "What the hell is this?" he demanded, his voice vibrating with barely contained rage. "You think you can just take her? You have no idea who you're dealing with."

I stood my ground, unflinching, and spoke calmly and sharply. "David deserves a chance to make things right. A real chance, not the kind I gave him before. This isn't about you, Frederick. It's not about me, either. It's about Jean and what she needs. I've been the one sabotaging her happiness, not him."

Frederick's eyes blazed. "You've made a huge mistake. I'll have every resource at my disposal hunting them down. If she's hurt—"

"—She won't be," I interrupted, my voice as cold as the ocean below. "But you'll never know if you don't give them this chance. If you're so sure you're the better man, then give David an hour. That's all I'm asking. One hour. Then you can call in your helicopters, the Coast Guard, whatever it takes to find them."

Frederick glared at me, his jaw tight, but I could see the hesitation. He didn't like being challenged, but I knew how to push the right buttons. I always did.

"One hour," he said finally, his voice low and dangerous.

"If anything happens to her, Beth, I swear to God, you'll be the one paying for it."

I nodded, keeping my expression unreadable. "Deal."

And with that, the game was set. David had sixty minutes to find whatever it was he and Jean had lost. I found that I had surprising confidence in his ability to do it. I had to because I'd watched his expression after he settled her in the boat—God, it was like watching a man see the sun for the first time after being trapped in darkness. He'd stared at her with a mix of longing and pain, and I knew that this was his last shot. He couldn't come back from this.

# Chapter Nine

*Jean*

The cold sea air stung my face as we sped away from the yacht, the motor of the boat roaring beneath us. I was drenched, furious, and my teeth chattered from more than just the chill of the water. I refused to look at David, gripping the side of the boat so tightly my knuckles were white. I couldn't believe what had just happened—what he and Beth had orchestrated.

David glanced over at me, his expression a mix of relief and regret that made my blood boil. He didn't say a word, probably sensing I was on the edge of losing it. Good, I thought bitterly. He should be scared.

The night was a blur of salt spray and engine noise. David kept his eyes fixed on the GPS console, steering us through the darkness with a ridiculous ease. I didn't care where we were going. I just wanted to get out of this boat, to scream at him, to demand answers, but the anger was so hot, so sharp in my throat that I couldn't even form words. All I could do was seethe, each wave that splashed over the boat feeding my fury.

I refused to ask where we were heading; I wouldn't give him the satisfaction. My silence was the only weapon I had left. He tried to catch my eye a couple of times, but I turned away, staring out into the endless stretch of black ocean, feeling trapped and betrayed. It wasn't just Beth who had shoved me over the edge—it was David, too, with schemes and his arrogance, thinking he could just sweep me away as if we could fix everything with a grand gesture.

After what felt like an eternity, we navigated into a small, hidden cove. It was serene, a world away from the chaos on the yacht. Moonlight reflected off the calm waters, and the place looked almost magical, like something out of a dream. But I wasn't fooled. I was still angry—so furious that it burned in my chest.

David cut the engine and pulled the key out, pocketing it as he hopped onto the dock. "Jean," he said softly, reaching out his hand as if expecting me to follow.

I glared at him, refusing to move. I wasn't going to make this easy for him.

When it became clear that I wasn't budging, David finished tying off the boat and climbed onto the dock, giving me one last look before heading to a seating area nearby. A firepit blazed in the center, casting a warm glow over the cozy arrangement of chairs and plush blankets. There was a small bar stocked with bottles, glasses neatly arranged, and a spread of food laid out on a low table. Stone steps cut into the hillside led up through lush vegetation, large solar lights styled like torches lighting the way up to a hidden house, just the hint of its roofline visible through the treetops.

It was all so perfectly prepared, so meticulously planned, and that only made my anger flare hotter. He'd gone to all this trouble to get me alone, to corner me like I was some problem he could solve with the right setting and a heartfelt apology.

I stayed on the boat for a while, refusing to move as I watched David settle himself near the fire. He leaned back, staring into the flames, giving me my space but not saying a word. Minutes ticked by, each one feeling like an hour. I knew he was waiting me out, giving me time to cool off. But that wasn't going to happen. Not tonight.

Finally, the stillness got to me. The silence between us was heavy, charged with everything left unsaid. I climbed out of the boat, my clothes still wet and clinging to me, and made my way to the seating area. I didn't sit next to him. I chose the furthest chair, keeping the firepit between us like a shield, but grateful for the warmth of the flames to dry my dress.

"You obviously think you can plead your case," I said, my voice dripping with sarcasm. "Do it, and then take me back."

David looked at me, his expression gentle but determined. "There's a change of clothes for you up in the house," he said, nodding toward the stairs. "I set it up so you'd be comfortable."

"I'm fine," I snapped, crossing my arms over my chest. "This isn't some romantic getaway, David."

He sighed and moved to the bar, pouring something into a glass. He didn't seem fazed by my anger. If anything, he wore the look of a man who'd been expecting this, who knew he'd have to work for every inch of forgiveness. He brought the drink over, holding it out to me. "It's just a drink, Jean. Take it."

I stared at the glass, feeling a surge of defiance, but then I grabbed it, draining it in one go. I hated that it tasted good, hated that he knew that my favorite was green apple vodka, that the trays of food on the nearby table were covered with appetizers that I would have ordered myself, and that everything had been planned so carefully. It made me feel like he'd been inside my head, rearranging things without permission.

David sat back down, watching me carefully. "I'm sorry," he began, his voice low and steady. "I'm sorry for every minute, every second I didn't see you. I didn't see your kindness, your intelligence, the beauty of your soul. I let so much bullshit cloud my vision. I let Beth manipulate me, and I let you down in every way that mattered."

I didn't respond, my jaw tight as I fought against the emotions that were building inside me. I didn't want to hear this. Not now, not here. But David continued, his voice raw and sincere.

"I never should've even considered that you had anything to do with what happened with the suit at the funeral home. That was on me, all of it. We should've been a team, Jean. You and me against the world. But I let Beth get between us, and that's my fault. I was weak, and I believed things I never should have."

My eyes burned, and I blinked hard, determined not to let him see me cry. But his words were breaking down every wall I'd built. I hated him for making me feel like this, for pulling me back into the past when all I wanted was to move forward.

David's voice wavered, and he looked away, his shoulders slumping slightly. "I'm so damn sorry I told you not to come to my father's funeral. You have no idea how much that haunts me, Jean. He cared about you so much. You meant more to him than most people ever did, myself included, and I took that away from you. I took away your chance to say goodbye."

Tears welled in my eyes despite my best efforts, and a choked sob escaped me. I'd loved David's father—he'd been kind to me. Losing him had been painful, but being barred from the funeral had felt like a betrayal I couldn't get over. Hearing David acknowledge that now, it cut deep.

"You're right," I said, my voice trembling. "You can't make that up to me. You took away something I can never get back."

David nodded, pain etched on his face. "I know, Jean. I know I can't ever fix that. But I'm telling you now—I see what I've done. I see how wrong I've been."

He reached out like he wanted to touch me, but I pulled back, the anger and hurt swirling inside me too much to bear. I waited for the apology I really wanted—for him to take back the day he'd fired me, to admit that it had been a mistake, that he'd thrown away something irreplaceable in Beth's manipulations. But the apology never came.

Instead, David stared into the fire, gathering his thoughts. When he finally spoke, his voice was softer, but no less determined. "I'm not sorry for firing you, Jean."

I recoiled, disbelief flooding my veins. "You're *not* sorry?" I demanded. "After everything you've put me through, you're not sorry for *that*?"

He held up his hands, placating. "Hear me out. You didn't deserve to lose your job. You were the best thing that ever happened to Shep and Son, and firing you was the absolute worst decision I've ever made. But Jean, look at where you are now. You have the brightest future ahead of you. Frederick Donelson sees you, really sees you, and he's giving you a once-in-a-lifetime opportunity to work with him, to be in a position where you call the shots. You're in control of your own destiny now."

I was shaking, my hands clenched into fists. "You think that makes it okay? You think that justifies what you did?"

David leaned forward, his eyes locked on mine. "I can't apologize for putting you on this path, because I believe in you more than I've ever believed in anything. You're brilliant, Jean. You deserve everything Frederick is offering you and more. And I'm asking you to let me be there—not as your boss, not as your partner, but as the no-good, dirty dog who doesn't even deserve to lick your feet."

I stared at him, stunned by his words.

He laughed, the sound edged with bitterness. "I know I'm a mess, Jean. I'm the mangiest mutt you've ever seen, but I swear to God, I will be devoted to you every second of every day. I will love you the way I should have from the moment I met you six years ago. I was blind, I was stupid, but I'm not anymore."

He slid off his chair and knelt in the sand, the firelight dancing across his face. My heart pounded as he reached into his pocket, pulling out a small velvet box. When he opened it, a stunning vintage tear-drop diamond ring sparkled inside, catching the glow of the flames. It was breathtaking—a family heirloom, no doubt, and it looked like something that had been passed down through generations.

"Jean," David said, his voice cracking with emotion. "I know I don't deserve you. I know I've messed up more times than I can count. But I love you. I love you more than anything, and I want to spend the rest of my life making it up to you. Will you marry me?"

I stood there, frozen, my mind reeling. It was everything I'd ever wanted to hear. It was too much, too fast, too loaded with everything that had gone wrong between us. David looked up at me, his eyes pleading, and I could see the sincerity there. But I could also see the desperation, the fear of losing me for good.

I hesitated, my breath catching in my throat. This was the moment—the point of no return. I could say yes and dive back into the chaos of loving David, or I could walk away and protect myself from ever feeling this hurt again.

The fire crackled, the ocean lapped softly at the shore, and David waited, his heart in his hands.

And I was left on the edge, teetering between love and self-preservation, with no idea which way to fall.

\*\*\*

*Beth*

*Six Months Later*

I stood barefoot in the sand, the sun setting over the Florida gulf, its light casting a warm, golden hue across the beach. The waves lapped gently at the shore, whispering secrets only the sea could keep. I glanced down at my feet, feeling the soft grains of sand nestle between my toes. The moment was surreal—a perfect blend of everything I'd hoped to create, and here it was, unfolding right before my eyes.

Jean's wedding. My sister's wedding. And it was glorious.

I'd been the planner of this whole affair, down to the last vintage glass soda bottle strung with twinkling lights around the altar. They caught the sun's rays just right, flickering like tiny stars as if they were hanging in a sky of their own. It had been a risky touch—one I wasn't sure Jean would go for, considering our history, but she'd laughed when she saw them. "You really went there," she said, her smile wide, eyes crinkling with a kind of genuine joy I hadn't seen in a long time.

Yes, I went there. I'd gone everywhere for Jean, and for once, I'd done it right.

Across the aisle, Frederick Donelson stood tall in a sharp navy suit. He caught my eye, a small smile playing on his lips, and I felt a thrill run through me. His gaze lingered, a silent acknowledgment of everything we'd been through to get here, and more importantly, of the something new that was blooming between us.

Frederick and I. Who'd have thought?

He was David's best man, and in a strange twist of fate, he'd become my...something. We hadn't labeled it yet, but whatever it was, it was good. Better than good. In a way, it felt like fate. Like all the missteps I'd taken had somehow led me to this sandy beach, under this wide-open sky, with Frederick nearby and Jean about to marry the man she'd loved for so long.

George, my half-brother and Jean's whole brother, was grinning like an idiot on the other side of Frederick—who looked like he'd just stumbled into the best day of his life. Jean's niece Mary was next to me, her little face a picture of absolute concentration as she adjusted her bouquet of roses. She was taking her bridesmaid duties seriously, which was fitting since she'd been talking about nothing but this wedding for weeks. Mary was almost bouncing on her toes in excitement, the sight of her happiness making me smile.

I couldn't believe we'd pulled this off. Jean had done the unexpected—choosing David over Frederick but still taking the job Frederick had offered. She'd walked that fine line, somehow managing to have both the career of her dreams and the love she'd never let go of. And in true Donelson fashion, Frederick had come through in ways none of us could've imagined. He'd not only saved Jean's job by offering her the publishing house position but had also swooped in to purchase Shep and Son when it was on the brink of collapse.

The company was a sinking ship, and everyone knew it. David's absence during his downward spiral had left a mess in its wake, but Frederick had seen an opportunity rather than a failure. He'd bought the company, saved everyone's jobs, and given the employees a choice: move to Florida and work on-site, enjoying the ocean views and sunshine, or stay in Elmburn and work remotely, with all expenses paid for training trips to Florida whenever they needed them. It was an olive branch, a lifeline, and everyone had grasped it eagerly. He was ruthless in business but fair, always thinking ten steps ahead.

And now, here we all were, on this private beach in Florida, miles from where everything had gone so wrong, but also right. The sand was soft, the ocean a gentle roar in the background, and above us, the sky was a painter's palette of colors, blending into one another like a dream.

Then there was the Elvis impersonator. Because, of course, there was. Jean's idea, not mine. After everything that had happened with the Elvis-lookalike back when she'd had her accident, she'd decided it was only fitting that he be the one to officiate today.

He was decked out in his rhinestone-studded white jumpsuit, complete with the cape and all, ready to take center stage with a cheeky grin. His pompadour was as high as his energy, and the sight of him almost made me burst out laughing. It was ridiculous and beautiful, just like life itself was starting to be.

Then Jean appeared, and every thought left my mind.

She was stunning. Breathtaking in a way that made the whole world feel like it had just hit pause. Her dress flowed around her like she was wrapped in a cloud, delicate lace and soft, cascading layers that moved with every step. She looked radiant, more beautiful than I'd ever seen her, and the expression on her face was a mix of nerves, excitement, and pure, unfiltered happiness.

David was standing at the altar, his eyes locked on her, and the love in his gaze was so palpable it almost hurt to witness. He looked at Jean like she was the sun and he'd spent his whole life in darkness. He had cleaned up well, ditching the disheveled look that had clung to him for weeks, and now he was every bit the man Jean had always seen in him, even when no one else could.

I watched as Jean walked down the aisle, every step measured, every movement graceful despite being barefoot on the soft beach sand. The wind caught the waves of her red hair, and the sun dipped lower, casting a halo around her. She was glowing—truly glowing. She'd made her choice, and standing there, witnessing this moment, I knew it was the right one.

My focus turned back to Frederick. There was a sadness in his eyes, but also something else—pride. He was watching Jean, the woman he'd offered everything to, walk down the aisle to another man. And yet, there was no bitterness, no jealousy. He was simply happy for her, happy that she had found what she was looking for. That she was following her heart, wherever it led.

Jean reached the altar, and as she took David's hand, the look they shared was the kind of thing that songs are written about. It was deep and intense, a love that had weathered every storm and come out stronger. I felt tears prick at the corners of my eyes, and for once, I didn't fight them. This was a moment worth feeling.

The Elvis impersonator cleared his throat, his deep voice carrying over the gentle sound of the waves. "Well, folks," he drawled, his smile wide and knowing. "We're gathered here today to witness a love story that's taken a few twists and turns, huh, but hey, that's what makes life worth living. So let's get this show on the road, shall we?"

Jean and David exchanged vows that were equal parts sweet, funny, and so undeniably them. David spoke first, his voice thick with emotion, promising to be Jean's greatest champion, her protector, and the man she deserved. He vowed to never take her for granted again, to cherish every moment, and to be better for her because she made him want to be better.

Jean's vows were raw, a perfect encapsulation of everything she'd been through, everything they'd survived. She talked about the long nights, the missed moments, the pain of loving someone from afar, and the joy of finding each other again. She promised to love him fiercely, to stand by him through every high and low, and to never let fear dictate her heart again. At the end, she slipped in a promise always to call to hear his voice, and never to text, drawing a snicker from those of us who knew the details.

When they exchanged rings, I couldn't help but glance at Frederick. His eyes were on the couple, a smile tugging at his lips. He'd given Jean the career of her dreams, and now he was giving her the space to live the life she wanted. He'd been gracious in every way that mattered, and the more I got to know him, the more I realized how rare that was.

The ceremony was brief, but it was everything it needed to be. When the Elvis officiant pronounced them husband and wife, the cheers erupted, loud and jubilant. David pulled Jean into his arms, kissing her like they were the only two people on the planet, and for a moment, I think they were.

I glanced at Frederick again, catching the soft look in his eyes. He reached for my hand as we recessed down the sandy aisle, lacing his fingers through mine, and I squeezed back, feeling the weight of everything lift, if only a little. We were on our own journey, one that was just beginning, but in that moment, everything felt possible.

The sun dipped below the horizon, and the sky deepened into a rich, velvety twilight. Lanterns flickered along the beach, and the first stars of the evening began to twinkle overhead. Jean and David pulled apart slightly on the dance floor, their foreheads resting together as they laughed softly, lost in their own world.

All around us, there was celebration, joy spilling over in every laugh, every tear, every smile. The past felt distant, like a bad dream we were all waking up from, and the future stretched out before us, bright and full of promise.

I took a deep breath, letting the salt air fill my lungs, and smiled. This was the kind of day you couldn't plan for, not really. It was priceless, full of heart, and, for the first time, more gratifying than any scheme even I could hatch.

Madeline Quinn is the pen name for a funeral director and embalmer who moonlights as an author in western North Dakota. She finds the same mix of art, science, and dedication required for funeral service to be essential for writing.